THE PHANTOM ROUNDABOUT
and other ghostly tales

By the same author

THE TEN TALES OF SHELLOVER
MORE TALES OF SHELLOVER
THE PHANTOM CYCLIST
THE PHANTOM FISHERBOY

Ruth Ainsworth

THE
PHANTOM
ROUNDABOUT

and other ghostly tales

Illustrated by Shirley Hughes

André Deutsch

First published 1977 by
André Deutsch Limited
105 Great Russell Street London WC1

Copyright © 1977 by Ruth Ainsworth
Illustrations © 1977 by Shirley Hughes
All rights reserved

Printed in Great Britain by
Cox and Wyman Ltd
London, Fakenham and Reading

ISBN 0 233 96788 5

45294

CHATHAM PUBLIC LIBRARY
BOOKMOBILE

Contents

The Phantom Roundabout 9
A Sprig of Rosemary 22
Give me my Bone 35
The Blood Stain 45
Twin Stars 60
Rock-a-bye-baby 73
The Captain's Cabin 84
The Sunset Call 100
Draw the Curtains 109
The White Pony 127
Lay them Straight 140
Through the Door 156

THE PHANTOM ROUNDABOUT
and other ghostly tales

The Phantom Roundabout

Silas always felt as if his life had been cut into two separate parts, young though he was. The first three years of the seven in which he had lived were misty and faraway, but magical. The last four, which were clear and sharp, were ordinary as bread-and-butter.

Silas had lived on a farm with his father and mother till he was three. Then both his parents were killed in a car accident, and he was taken to live with his Uncle Walter and Aunt Ellen in a small house in a crowded, smoky town.

Silas remembered little of those early years but that little was far from ordinary. He remembered his mother as someone with a cloud of fair hair and a sweet scent, and his father as someone of immense height and strength, who sometimes swung him up on to the back of Blossom, the shire horse, and held him there while Blossom drank from the water trough. These memories were fostered by the photograph of his mother which stood by his bed, and a snapshot of himself on Blossom's back. Without these reminders, they might have been overlaid by the events of the present.

But the memory of Blossom was kept green in another way. Every year, a fair came to the town and was set up on some waste land not far from the house where Silas lived. He could hear the music of the roundabout as he lay in bed at night. Best of all, Uncle Walter took him to the fair on Saturday afternoon, when he did not go to work.

The roundabout was not very up-to-date and the machine that worked it left much to be desired. The horses on which the children rode were shaped like real horses, differing in colour and expression. The first time Silas had a ride, his uncle said: 'Which will you have? Hurry up! They're all much of a muchness.'

But to Silas they were completely individual. Some looked sly – others even vicious – some were proud and others were friendly. They had their names painted on a band on their foreheads.

'What is this one called, Uncle?'

'Pegasus. Hurry up and make up your mind. We haven't all day. Which shall it be?'

'Pegasus, please,' said Silas, and he was promptly lifted on to the painted saddle.

In the brief interval before the roundabout began to turn,

Silas examined Pegasus. He was a particularly fiery, spirited steed, with coal black mane and tail, and a red saddle. There was a tuft of hair springing up between his ears, which were slightly bent back, as if to hear the voice of his rider. His eyes showed their whites in a curious manner. Then the music started up and Pegasus gathered his strength and leapt forward, Silas clinging fast to the brass rod that tethered each horse in his place. The music was rousing and martial, and Silas pretended he was riding at the head of his men, leading a charge. He felt Pegasus's sides, warm and throbbing, and saw the breath from his dilated nostrils. It was a wonderful experience.

When his uncle lifted him down, he was in a daze of happiness and could hardly answer the inquiries as to whether he had enjoyed himself.

'Another ride, please,' he begged. 'I don't want any pocket-money for weeks – for months – you can keep it. But I must ride Pegasus again. I must!'

Silas was usually such a quiet little boy that his uncle was impressed by his enthusiasm.

'All right,' he agreed. 'You're a good little chap.'

The next ride was even better. Silas felt warmth coming from Pegasus's painted sides and even heard his laboured breath. His ears twitched and his mane felt coarse and living as Silas twined his fingers in it. The ride was quickly over but he had experienced peril and excitement as he rode at the head of his men, whispering encouragements and endearments into the delicate, pointed ears.

Something kept him from asking for a third turn. He did not want to push his luck too far. He had had a great deal.

The fair stayed for two nights only. As he lay in bed, he listened to the music and in his dreams he rode Pegasus once more.

It was twelve months before the fair visited the town again, but in some ways it seemed less. Silas dreamed regularly that he was riding his beloved Pegasus and he often tried to draw him. One of his efforts was so successful that it was pinned up on the wall at school. His teacher told him that Pegasus had been a winged horse. It only needed this to complete the picture in his mind. Silas had often wished that he could fly, but a flying horse was far better. It was nearer possibility.

The second visit to the fair was even more memorable than the former one. He was bigger and stronger himself, and had saved his pocket-money for weeks in preparation. But he was not considered old enough to go to the fair alone. He had to wait for Uncle Walter to take him. This time the fair was coming for one night only.

Silas watched his uncle eating his tea of sausage and mash with an unwavering gaze. Surely he would not want a *third* cup of tea – but he did. Not a cigarette as well – but he wanted that, too.

'Uncle,' he said desperately, seeing him stoop down to unlace his boots. 'Uncle – the fair!'

'Good heavens, so it is. The music ought to have reminded me. It's loud enough.'

'Uncle, I could go alone. Really I could. I'm seven and a bit.'

'You could do no such thing,' said his aunt quickly. 'A little shrimp like you. You'd get lost. You'd come to some harm in those rough crowds.'

'O.K.,' said Uncle Walter. 'Off we go. Just one ride, mind you.'

Silas pressed his pocket-money into his uncle's hand without a word.

His uncle counted it carefully.

'They say money talks. This says you can have – let me see

– six rides, unless they've gone up since last year. You'll be all right if I go and have a try at the shooting gallery? I fancied myself with a rifle when I was a young man.'

'Yes, Uncle. I'll be all right.'

At first he could not see Pegasus and then a low whinny caught his ear. Pegasus slightly turned his head and moved his ears, welcoming his old friend. He was not as glossy as he had been a year ago, and some red paint was chipped off his saddle. Also his mane had lost a few tufts. But he was unmistakable, proud and spirited and full of life.

The charges had gone up as his uncle had feared, but his money paid for four rides, each a marvellous experience. The music was the same, but it no longer filled Silas with dreams of military glory. This time he rode over open country, jumping hedges and ditches and gates. Sometimes Pegasus's hoofs floundered in mud, and sometimes they rang on frozen ground. Clouds sailed by – branches swayed – birds wheeled – while they galloped in perfect freedom.

By the end of the fourth round Pegasus was sweating slightly and his mighty chest heaved. Silas's pale cheeks were flushed and he, too, was short of breath.

'Till next year, my darling,' he whispered, as he gave Pegasus a farewell pat and stroked his soft nose. 'Don't forget me.'

Uncle Walter took him home, full of grumbles about the fair.

'It's going down-hill fast,' he complained. 'The blessed rifles were all cock-eyed. I couldn't bring down a thing. I wanted a pink jug for the mantelpiece,' he explained to his wife, 'but not a hope. Other people were grousing, too. No prizes worth having – no sideshows worth paying for – everything double the money – and the place so shabby. Torn canvas flapping in the wind. I was real fed up. How were the roundabouts,

Silas? Did you get your favourite horse? Wasn't he the worse for wear?'

'He was as beautiful as ever, Uncle. Beautiful as a dream,' he added under his breath.

The following year the fair never came, though Silas looked for the notices on hoardings and lamp-posts.

'Packed up, I shouldn't wonder,' said his uncle cheerfully. 'It was on its way out last time.'

Silas suffered in silence, thankful that Pegasus still came to him in sleep, perhaps not as often, but just as clearly. Their midnight rides were as thrilling as ever and Pegasus often went so fast that he lived up to his namesake, the horse with wings. The next year the fair still made no appearance but Pegasus's dream visits continued. Then the next year the fair re-appeared in all its glory.

NEW! STUPENDOUS! GIGANTIC ATTRACTIONS! BETTER! BRIGHTER! FASTER! FUN FOR ALL!

screamed the notices.

All the old favourites and many new ones, said the small print.

Silas was now ten and felt that he was on the way to being grown-up. He had a bicycle, second-hand, it was true, but it went well and his aunt was not too fussy about where he went and when he got back. That is, as long as he was home well before dark.

On the first evening of the fair's re-appearance, Silas was there in good time, seeking the roundabout. The mechanism had been changed and the music was no longer martial. But worst of all, the painted horses had gone with the old tunes. In their place were cars and aeroplanes. Silas had no inclination to try either of these. His disappointment was intense. He felt a lump in his throat and his eyes smarted. He turned away and spent all his carefully hoarded money on the dodge 'em cars.

Then, before he left the fairground, he went back to the roundabout. Yes, in spite of almost everything new, the man in charge was the same, a little older and smarter, but the same.

'Where are the old horses?' asked Silas.

'Oh, scrapped. Done for. We must move with the times like everyone else. No boy worth his salt would prefer a horse to these magnificent cars and planes. This is a mechanical age. Don't you agree?'

'What did you mean by scrapped?' asked Silas. 'Do you mean burned?'

'Maybe they ought to have been burned – they're a lot of rubbish. But the old roundabout with the horses is stored in a barn not far from here. Somehow, I hadn't the heart to let them go. I wondered if they might come in handy, one day. I don't quite know how, I confess. I felt a bit sentimental. My father owned them and it was my first job, when I was a nipper like you, to help him. In the winter, I used to touch up the horses, re-do their manes and faces.'

'Did you touch up Pegasus? You did him very well.'

'First time I've had my handiwork admired. He was the black fellow, wasn't he, with the red saddle? Oh yes, I touched him up many times.'

'Where is the barn, sir, exactly?' Silas tried to keep his voice flat and cool.

'At a hamlet called Whitestones, about twenty miles away. A farmer let me have a tumbledown barn for nothing. But wait a minute, why do you want to know? There's enough vandalism goes on in the world. You're not up to any mischief, are you? You *look* quiet enough.'

'I mean no harm,' said Silas quickly. 'You see I used to ride on Pegasus when I was a little kid. Quite took my fancy. I'm glad you didn't burn him.'

He moved away, his mind busy. He must see Pegasus again. He must find Whitestones on the map. First, he must find a map. His bicycle had given him freedom to carry out these plans.

There was no map in his uncle's house, but the public library proved helpful. He found Whitestones and drew the route on a piece of paper. When an opportunity came, he would go there. It must be a fine day, or his aunt would fuss about getting wet. He mustn't rouse any suspicions. He'd waited three years so he could wait a little longer. He'd heard a proverb: 'Everything comes to him who waits'. But he was not certain that Pegasus would come to him. Anyhow, he was going to Pegasus, so that should be all right.

The next Sunday was sunny and he got up early and pumped up his tyres, took some bread and cheese and an apple, filled a bottle with water and packed up his fishing rod. This last was a blind as he had no intention of using it. Then he left a note on the kitchen table, weighed down with the bread knife.

Dear Auntie,
   It is such a lovely day that I'm going for a ride on my bike. I've taken my fishing rod and some food. Don't worry. I'll be home long before dark.
                                       Silas.

It was a blue summer morning, with a few fleecy clouds blowing. The roads were empty. The way to the sea, which might have been crowded, lay in a different direction. Silas seldom went into the country in the ordinary way, but he enjoyed all he saw, the black and white cows, the sheep, and the odd dog or cat going quietly about its business. Now if he could have a kitten of his own – but he knew his aunt's views on cats. 'Nasty sly creatures leaving their fur everywhere and sharpening their claws on the furniture.'

He had dreamed once during the previous night and then not about Pegasus. Or not really about Pegasus. He dreamed he was in a field and nearby was a barn, almost falling to pieces. But it had a new roof of corrugated iron. From inside came the sound of a horse whinnying and the stamp of a horse's hoofs. He woke before he had tried the door.

When he reached Whitestones it was eleven o'clock. He had been cycling for nearly three hours and his legs ached. He ate the bread and cheese and had a drink from his water bottle. Then he walked down the village street, pushing his bicycle. A woman was sweeping her front path. No, she didn't know of any local barn where disused roundabouts might be stored. She looked kind and did not seem surprised at his question, which gave Silas courage.

He asked two more people with the same result. There were very few people about. Perhaps they are all in church, he thought, having heard the bells ringing earlier. Then he came across a boy a few years older than himself, tinkering with a moped. He looked interested at the question and stood up, spanner in hand.

'You're in luck. I happen to know. The shed's about a mile away, near Orchard Farm. You'll know the place because it was burnt down a few years ago and the farmer left. The shed is beyond the orchard. I suppose they once packed apples in it, but that was when I was a little 'un. I looked through a crack in the door last autumn, when I was pinching apples. It was dark and dusty but I saw something that might be what you're looking for.'

'Thanks a lot.'

Silas got on his bicycle and rode up a long, gradual hill. At the top were the blackened remains of a building and nearby rows and rows of apple trees. No one took care of them and the brambles and weeds were thick on the ground. Here and there was a drift of creamy apple blossom. He left his bicycle by a stone gate post and walked through the orchard, finding it heavy going. There, in the next field, was the building he had seen in his dream, unpainted, ricketty, but with a corrugated iron roof gleaming in the sun. A flock of pigeons took flight as he approached.

There was a rusty padlock on the door, but he soon saw that the door was falling to pieces. A brisk tug removed a loose plank and he slipped through, being small and thin for his age. The gap let in a shaft of sunlight.

The roundabout was smaller than he had remembered and the horses were smaller too, and less attractive. He climbed over the rubbish that cluttered the floor, the darkness pierced by endless shafts of light that found their way through the wide cracks. There was Snowdrop, the white horse. And Warrior, the grey one. And Magpie, the piebald one. But when he had completed the circle he had seen all the horses he remembered, except Pegasus. Then he saw a gap – and empty brass rod, very tarnished, connected only with the canopy above. That was Pegasus's empty place.

His disappointment was overwhelming. He had often feared he might not find the barn, but once that was identified, he never doubted that Pegasus would be safe inside, waiting for him.

He touched the wooden, dusty nose of one of the horses. It felt cold. He slipped out the way he had come, wiping his dusty hands on his trousers. He began to eat the apple to comfort himself. Then he heard the eager whinny of a horse.

He looked up and there, in the next field, was a black horse, galloping towards the gate. Silas ran too. A minute later he was stroking the soft black nose and looking into the nervous, rolling eyes he knew so well.

'Pegasus, my darling. You're more beautiful than ever.' He gently pulled the tuft of hair between Pegasus's ears, fondling him and stroking him as he talked.

'Have half my apple. Oh, you've left me a bite? Very well. We'll share it. Now you can have the core.'

Pegasus pressed against the gate, alongside it, whinnying and gently tapping with a front hoof, as if impatient. He put his head over the gate and nibbled Silas's anorak.

'You want me to get on your back? Of course, I will. I didn't understand at first. I'll climb on the gate as you suggested. That's fine. I'm safe as houses. I've never been so happy in my life. This is just like my dreams, only better because it's true. Perhaps you dreamed the same dreams and they've both come true together? Is that it?'

Pegasus began to move gently, then changed to a trot – then a canter – then a full gallop. The ground flew beneath his pounding hoofs. Silas felt like a king – a god. Then, as they approached the far hedge, the blue sky swung down to meet them, and the grass flew up at the same time. A black curtain fell across Silas's eyes. He saw flashing lights like the lights of the fair, and heard loud music. Then all was silence.

The next thing Silas saw, when he opened his eyes, was a bright red blanket, and he heard a soft voice saying:

'That's better, Silas. Lie quite still. Everything will be all right.'

'Where am I?'

'You're in hospital and I am a nurse.'

'Why am I in hospital? I'm not ill.'

'You had an accident and bumped your head. You'll soon be better.'

Presently he put up his hand and felt an unfamiliar turban of bandages.

'Try to sleep. Your aunt will be coming this afternoon. She comes to see you every day.'

He closed his eyes and slept.

A day later, he was well enough to ask more questions and listen to the answers.

'You were found in a field by a hedge,' said his aunt, 'twenty miles from here. Whatever were you doing, Silas, so far away?'

In time, Silas explained his search for the old roundabout, but he never mentioned Pegasus's name. That was his secret, his dream. His aunt would be sure to think that the bump on his head had turned him silly.

'There was one thing no one could understand,' she went on. 'You were lying near a ditch, where water lay, and on the wet ground there were prints of horses' hoofs. The owner of the field says he never let it for grazing. Do you remember a horse?'

'No. I don't remember.'

But he did. He never forgot the last, wild ride on his winged steed. Pegasus must have flown away, leaving him earthbound.

Life goes on, and boys with concussion and ten stitches in their head leave hospital and even go back to school. Silas never dreamed of Pegasus again but he never forgot him, in the same way that he never forgot Blossom.

What nobody expected was that he should grow up, still small and thin and pale, and become a famous jockey. His greatest success was to win the Derby on a horse called Pegasus, a black horse full of spirit. He had a way with horses, everyone said. A magical touch.

A Sprig of Rosemary

Joanna had the smallest garden you can possibly imagine. It wasn't really a garden at all – it was a small, paved yard, so small that when the umbrella clothes' drier was hung with clothes, there was barely room to squeeze round it.

But when Joanna's mother was not doing any washing and the clothes' drier was folded together, then the yard – what there was of it – was all Joanna's.

She certainly made the most of it. She could skip if she stayed in one spot, so she stayed in one spot. She collected snails from the walls and tried to persuade them to race across the paving-stones. The winner was rewarded with a bit of cabbage leaf, or the green frond off a carrot.

Her two dolls, Milly and Molly, had tea-parties, using the blue, enamel tea-set that had been Joanna's mother's, and eating, if they were lucky, some biscuit crumbs and a few raisins. Milly was greedy and had to be scolded for eating more than her share. Molly, on the other hand, was faddy and had to be coaxed.

Joanna's little house was squeezed between two bigger ones. The next door house had a garden shaped like an 'L' which Joanna could look at if she stood on a kitchen chair and looked over the wall. At one of the upper windows, an old lady sat, day in and day out, watching, watching all that Joanna did down below. Occasionally, if it were hot and the window were open at the bottom, she waved a white, lace handkerchief.

Then Joanna waved back and she made the dolls wave too. The old lady's name was Mrs Raven.

One day, Joanna's mother called her indoors. She was holding a letter in her hand.

'Here's a note from Mrs Raven,' said her mother, 'and it's about you. She says she often watches you and wonders if you would care to play in her garden. This is what she says:

It would give me pleasure to have a child playing in my garden again, where no child has played for many years. Would Joanna care to play there sometimes? Let her slip in whenever she wishes. She may pick any flowers she likes and amuse herself how she pleases. Mr Shaw, the gardener, comes every Tuesday, so she will have to play at home that day.

The side door is unlocked till dusk and she may come and go as she pleases. There is no need to ask. She will always be welcome.

Yours sincerely,
Evelina Raven.

'May I go, mother?'

'Will you like being all alone there?'

'It will be the same as being alone here. I shall be only just through the wall. If you call me, I shall hear. And if I call you, you'll hear, too. May I go now, this very minute?'

'You are in a hurry to get away. Let me brush your hair, and you'd better wash your face, as well.'

Joanna never forgot her first day in the next door garden. It was hot and still, and the scent of the flowers was strange and unusual. Mr Shaw was only interested in flowers as there were no cabbages or potatoes anywhere, only some strawberries under nets, and some raspberry canes. There were flowers of every colour and kind. Lilies and little low pansies. Tall sweet peas. White and yellow daisies. Roses and plants that smelled sweetly when crushed between the finger and thumb. But she did not find out about these till later.

At first Joanna dared hardly pick a blade of grass, but she remembered what the letter said and soon ventured to gather a few roses for her mother. Then she collected fragrant leaves to tear up small and mix with water in a glass bottle. This she called: 'making scent'.

At eleven o'clock each morning – Joanna soon learned to listen for the chiming of the clock – a lady in an overall came through the French window and placed a tray on a stone bench. There was a glass of milk on the tray and two biscuits.

'With Mrs Raven's compliments,' said the lady.

Joanna began to look forward to the tray, the biscuits were so delicious. They were homemade, not from a shop. Sometimes they were decorated with cherries, sometimes nuts, sometimes a dab of icing. She ate them slowly, not wasting a crumb. Milly and Molly watched her hungrily.

When Joanna grew used to the next door garden, she began to enjoy herself even more. She no longer started if a branch creaked, or looked over her shoulder if a bird flew out of a bush. She even forgot about Mrs Evelina Raven at her upper window, unless she chanced to look that way and see the flutter of the white handkerchief. Then she waved back and smiled.

The first time she saw the other child was on a sunny day, when the roses were in bloom. She had filled her little basket with fallen petals, and was trying to fix a flower in Milly and Molly's hair.

'You're Japanese dolls now,' she said. Then she looked up

and saw another girl standing by a tree-trunk, very straight, very thin, wearing a white pinafore. She knew at once it was a pinafore from old-fashioned pictures. The girl had one hand on the bark of the tree, and in the other she was holding a white stick.

Joanna went towards her.

'I'm Joanna and I'm allowed to play here. I live next door.'

'I'm Rosemary. I don't know if I'm allowed here or not, but I used to know this garden well.'

'Was it your garden?'

'Yes. In a way.'

'Either it was or it wasn't,' said Joanna. 'Like black or white.'

'But that's not a distinction to me,' said the girl with a smile. 'I can't tell the difference between black and white, and never could. Except in dreams,' she added.

'Then you must be—' Joanna broke off and a blush spread over her freckles.

'Yes, I am. I'm blind. Quite, quite blind. Didn't you guess?'

'No, I didn't. Your eyes are wide open. I thought blind people had their eyes closed.'

'No,' said Rosemary, 'dead people have their eyes shut. Blind people can have them open.'

'Would you like to smell my scent? It's only home-made, so it doesn't smell like real perfume.'

'Yes, I would.' Rosemary sniffed delicately and said, as she sniffed:

'I smell balm and thyme and cotton lavender. And I think basil.'

'I don't know if you're right or wrong, because I don't know the names of most of the things I picked. You know all about the garden and its plants. How did you learn, without seeing them?'

'I had a wonderful mother,' said Rosemary, 'who made this garden for me and planted every sweet-smelling herb she could find. She took me round the garden every day and I touched and smelled them all. In the end, I knew them as well as I knew my own bedroom. It seemed to me they were different at different times of the day. Specially fresh in the early morning. Stronger at noon. Best of all in the evening. I've wandered round the garden in the moonlight in my nightgown, breathing it in.'

'You must have looked like a ghost,' said Joanna.

'Why do you say that?' Rosemary's fingers gripped her arm, and she sounded startled. 'Why do you say that word?'

'I didn't mean to upset you. I just meant that anyone in a white nightgown, wandering about in a garden in the moonlight, would look ghostly. That's all I meant.'

'Yes, I understand,' said Rosemary. 'But I must go now. I'll come again tomorrow. Goodbye, Joanna.'

'Goodbye.' Joanna watched her intently, but lost sight of her among the greenery. Her white pinafore glimmered and faded, like a fade-out in a film.

The next day, when Joanna arrived in the garden, Rosemary was there already.

'I've been round very carefully,' said Rosemary, 'and there's not a sprig of my name plant anywhere. And there was once. I'll show you where it used to grow.'

Rosemary took her hand (how cold her fingers are, thought Joanna) and with the outstretched white cane in the other, she led her unhesitatingly to a circle of crazy-paving bordered with plants.

'Here's the cotton lavender. Here's where it ought to be, between the lavender and the bergamot. I suppose it died. But no one told me. I should have guessed as it's my name flower. "Rosemary for remembrance", Mother used to say.'

'Would it help me to remember my lessons?' asked Joanna. 'That would be useful. We have to learn a list of spellings and be tested on Tuesdays. It makes me hate Tuesdays,' she added.

'I don't think rosemary could help you to learn spellings. It might help you to remember something you once knew.'

'That doesn't sound so useful,' said Joanna doubtfully. 'Most of the important things seem to be happening now. Perhaps it's different when you're older.'

'It's different for me,' said Rosemary. 'All my important things happened in the past. Except, of course, meeting you,' she added gently. 'That's very important.'

Sometimes Joanna forgot that Rosemary couldn't see, she joined so easily in any game that Joanna suggested. They often

A SPRIG OF ROSEMARY

played with the dolls, and Milly and Molly led a more adventurous life than they had up till now. They became famous explorers, and had narrow escapes at least twice a day. They were threatened by crocodiles – poisoned arrows – quicksands – hostile tribes – snake bites.

Rosemary was just as good in less thrilling roles, such as a doctor when Milly and Molly caught the measles, a schoolmistress when they went to school, and a ring-master when they joined a circus.

'I never guessed you were blind at the beginning,' said Joanna one day. 'And I often forget you are now.'

'Didn't you see my white stick? All blind people carry a white stick.'

'Yes, but somehow – it didn't mean you were blind. It seemed more like a wand. A magician's wand. It still does.'

'It's almost like a wand to me,' admitted Rosemary, 'because I have freedom to explore when it's in my hand. I'm lost without it.'

While the friendship between the two girls grew closer and warmer, Joanna didn't talk about her new friend to her mother, though she usually told her everything, as naturally as breathing. She realized, soon after their first meeting, that she wanted to keep Rosemary a secret. It had happened in the early days, when her mother had said to her:

'I saw you from the bedroom window this morning. You were talking to yourself, and laughing. It looked queer.'

'It wasn't queer, Mother, I was talking to Rosemary, and she often makes me laugh.'

'Rosemary who?' asked her mother quickly.

'Oh, I don't know her other name. I don't know even if she's got another name. She's just someone very very nice I play with.'

Her mother seemed relieved. 'Oh, an imaginary friend.

You used to have them when you were younger. Aren't you outgrowing these pretend people?'

'I'm not out-growing Rosemary. She's older than me, or I think she is, and very sensible. You'd approve.' That was the only time she had ever mentioned Rosemary to anyone.

Rosemary had a habit of disappearing when the tray with the milk and biscuits was laid on the stone seat. She vanished among the bushes, without a leaf stirring or a twig cracking. She never reappeared till the tray was removed.

At first, Joanna saved a biscuit for her, but she so plainly didn't want it, though she refused politely.

'Eat it yourself,' she said. 'I've outgrown biscuits.'

'I shall never outgrow these biscuits,' said Joanna, licking the icing off with her tongue before she took her first, half-moon bite. 'They are my favourite.'

The only cloud in Rosemary's clear sky was the absence of the rosemary bush. Never a day passed without her lingering by the cotton lavender and the bergamot, feeling with her free hand, and bending to smell, but all in vain.

'It worries you, doesn't it?' said Joanna sympathetically. 'It not being there, I mean.'

'Yes it does. If I could smell it again, and touch it, I'm sure I could remember something I've forgotten.'

'Supposing it's something sad?' said Joanna.

'I want to remember it anyhow, sad or happy. It's part of me. I want to be complete. You're not a whole person if your memory has a gap in it.'

Joanna made up her mind she would somehow get hold of a rosemary bush and ask Mr Shaw, the gardener, to plant it in place of the old one. But how? She had no idea how to begin. But where there's a will there's a way. She decided to ask help from her father, who would be less likely to ask awkward questions than her mother.

'Daddy, will you please buy me a rosemary bush? Quite a tiny baby one will do. It'll grow.'

'It won't grow in *this* garden,' said her father, firmly. 'Just a waste of money.'

He put his pipe back in his mouth, and opened the paper.

'I don't want it for this garden. I'm not as silly as all that!' said Joanna. 'No, I want it for Mrs Raven's garden, where I go and play.'

'She's rich enough to buy her own rosemary bushes,' said her father, 'but she's been very kind to you, I must say. All right, I'll see what I can do.'

Joanna heaved a sigh of relief. No awkward questions. No cross-examination. Just that re-assuring: 'I'll see what I can do.'

A few days later, her father gave her something soggy, wrapped up in newspaper.

'I got this from a chap at work,' he said. 'He's a great gardener. Says it's the wrong time of year for it to strike, but they're unpredictable things. I said I'd like it, right or wrong time. Is that O.K.?'

'Daddy, you're an angel. I'll take it across for Mr Shaw to plant now. It's Tuesday, so he'll be there.'

She ran out of the house and through the side door. Mr Shaw was putting his tools away. He was a gruff, whiskery old man, with red-rimmed eyes. She was rather frightened of him.

'Please, Mr Shaw, will you plant this rosemary for me? It might live. Anyhow, it's got a better chance of living if *you* plant it. I'll show you the place.'

She indicated the place between the cotton lavender and the bergamot, and fled, her heart pounding.

'That's a queer little lass,' said Mr Shaw to himself, taking a hand fork out of the shed. 'But I'll do what she asks for the sake of that other one. She reminds me of her, in a way. Same clear voice and light step like a bird.'

The next day Joanna visited the garden early. There was the rosemary, with its spiky, dark green leaves, looking hearty, firmed down in the wet soil. Mr Shaw had done his work well. A few minutes later, Rosemary joined her, silently, as always.

'Rosemary, can you see – I mean smell – do you notice anything different just here?'

The white stick inched along like an exploring finger. Then its owner bent down.

'It's rosemary. A little young rosemary. Oh Joanna, how kind of you. I've longed for one for ages.'

She pinched a sprig and smelt her fingers. She broke off a leaf and bit it delicately. Her face was transfigured – but was it extreme pleasure or extreme pain? Joanna took her hand in hers. It was colder than ever. Then Rosemary began speaking:

'Now I remember. It all comes back. I was walking along a cliff path with Mother. There was so much to smell and enjoy and hear. The bees on the flowers, the gulls crying overhead. It was a lovely spot because it had once been a garden – only it had been neglected for years and years and gone wild. But some of the garden flowers lived on among the wild ones, among the gorse bushes and the wild thyme and the clover. Then, I was sure I smelt rosemary. Perhaps I trod on it and bruised it with my foot. I stepped aside and bent down to pick a sprig – and the cliff crumbled away. Someone screamed louder than the seagulls – and I fell down, down, down. But I never reached the bottom. Sometimes I think I'm falling still, as one does in a dream.'

That morning the tray was not brought out and neither was Mrs Raven at her window. She hadn't been there for several days. When the clock had finished chiming eleven, Joanna looked in vain at the French door, and then raised her eyes to the bedroom window. Mrs Raven had come back. She was not sitting in her chair, as usual, but was standing up and leaning out, waving her lace handkerchief.

Joanna waved back.

'It's Mrs Raven,' she said to Rosemary. 'I haven't seen her lately.'

Rosemary turned her face upward, her dark eyes not blank and wandering, but bright with recognition.

'Mother! Mother!' she cried. 'Mother, I'm coming!'

Joanna felt the thin, cold fingers slip from her grasp and at the same time she saw the figure of Mrs Raven fade from the window. Then the garden was emptier and quieter than she had ever known it. The friendly ghost, whom she had learned to love, had joined that other ghost who had been waiting for her. She ran home, bewildered and upset, trying to understand.

That evening, the letter-box clicked and her mother picked an envelope off the mat. She opened it and read aloud:

'It's from Mrs Raven's housekeeper,' she said.

> I am writing to tell you that Mrs Raven died suddenly this morning, at eleven o'clock. She was a kind mistress and I shall miss her. She often said what pleasure it gave her to see your little girl playing in the garden. Her own little girl died at about the same age, through a tragic accident.

'Well, we never know what's round the corner,' said her mother. 'Here today, gone tomorrow. When did you see Mrs Raven last, Joanna? You told me she often waved to you.'

'Some time ago,' said Joanna. But she thought to herself; 'Only this morning. Only this morning at eleven.'

The house next door was sold and the new people built an extension into the garden. A studio, it was thought. They gave parties there. They made the wall higher which darkened Joanna's tiny yard even more.

Joanna grew old enough to go alone to the local park and play with her friends. Her mother was pleased that she no longer talked to herself or had make-believe companions. Later still, when she studied Hamlet at school, she came across Ophelia's lines: 'Rosemary, that's for remembrance.'

'But I don't need rosemary to help me to remember,' she said to herself. 'I shall never forget. Never in my life.'

Give me my Bone

Julian collected stamps. Norah collected pressed wild flowers. Timmy, the youngest in the family, had tried both. He found the stamp mounts impossible to manage. They stuck to everything except the right thing – to the table, to each other and to his fingers. He enjoyed gathering wild flowers and looking them up in the flower book, which was more attractive than a stamp catalogue. Then his interest flagged. Pressing them between newspapers, under a pile of books, was all very well, but his mother kept moving the books to dust or vacuum as the case might be, or he forgot about them. When he remembered, the result was brittle and faded.

But his was a collecting family and he felt left out, with a father who collected coins, and a mother who collected pewter jugs. Then, by chance, he hit on the perfect collecting hobby. He would collect bones.

He received little support from his family, who referred to his treasures as dirty – smelly – disgusting – or gruesome. But once his mind was made up, these insults had no power to wound. After a while, he scarcely heard them.

The very first bone was a wish-bone from a chicken, which suddenly struck him as being interesting and worth preserving. He resisted all Norah's efforts to pull it with him, and he spent some time washing and scraping it. It paid for the trouble. Other wish-bones came his way and it almost seemed as though he might become a collector of wish-bones. But this was not to be.

The next bone he found on a country walk. It was, or so he thought, a typical bone, with a knob at each end and a smooth shaft in between. Washing easily removed the clinging soil. There was something about its bleached appearance, its pure whiteness, that attracted him, as did the wonderful glossy, smooth texture. He rubbed it between his fingers with the pleasure that rubbing a pebble or a sea-shell gave.

From that time, slowly but surely, the bone collection grew. Some bones, though not his favourites, came from the remains on dinner plates. He acquired a tiny one like a fan, so delicate it seemed to let the light through, and another with fragile ribs like the strings of a miniature harp. But the best ones were found out of doors, bleached by sun and wind, preserved in soil like ancient pottery in an archaeological dig.

Once, when out walking, he found a whole dead sheep. It had slipped down a gryke in the limestone, some time ago, and its flesh had rotted away, or been eaten by carrion-crows or other predators. He did not react as strongly to this wealth of bones as might be expected. There were too many of them. They seemed still connected with their once living owner. Disquieting questions rose in his mind. Did the sheep live long after it fell? Did it break its neck, or only, perhaps, its leg? Did it starve slowly to death? He toyed with the notion of trying to reach the skull with the empty eye-sockets and rows of teeth. But he did not pursue it.

'You're really the best in the family, Tim,' said his father, one day. 'Julian is always wanting to write away for expensive stamps, or he needs a new album. Even Norah wants to buy a flower-press she saw advertised, as if newspaper wasn't good enough, and I hardly dare let your mother loose in an antique shop. While you need nothing that costs anything, except effort, and your own effort at that.'

'What about you, Daddy? Isn't collecting coins expensive?'

'I must admit, when I open a dealer's catalogue, I'm sorely tempted. And occasionally I fall.'

That year, the family went to Ireland for part of the children's school holidays. It suited everyone. The people were so kind – the donkeys so tame – the fields so green – the food so good. Norah added to her flower collection daily. They toured the west coast and the children wished they were tinkers and could live in a caravan and travel wherever their fancy led them.

Once, when walking along a lonely strip of coast, they came upon a ruined church on the edge of the cliffs. The churchyard was fast slipping into the sea below and some coffins had come apart, revealing their contents. Here were bones in profusion. It was Timmy's first experience of human bones, such as made up his own body.

'What do you think of this?' asked Julian, stooping to pick a detached finger.

'Horrible!' said Norah. 'Let's go on quickly.'

'We mustn't disturb any of the skeletons, poor things,' said their mother.

'They couldn't *know* we were disturbing them,' said Tim.

'No, I don't suppose they could, poor souls. But they were buried in hallowed ground and people who loved them may have been comforted to think of them lying in this peaceful spot. We'll not spoil their belief.'

'The sea'll get them soon enough,' said Norah. 'The cruel, crawling sea.'

They walked on farther down the cliff and Timmy saw a single bone protruding from the crag. It was not obviously a part of the churchyard and there were no signs of a coffin. He quickly picked it up and put it in his rucksack. When they returned to the farmhouse where they were staying that night, he put it at the bottom of his suitcase. He did not feel guilty over his find, but he preferred to keep it private. It was his own bone and his own business what he did with it.

The collection of bones was housed in various places. At first, Timmy spread them on the wide window-sill in his bedroom. Later, he laid them on a piece of black velvet, cut off an old skirt of his mother's. They looked particulary impressive, white and gleaming, against the dark background. But the collection grew and of course the velvet didn't. It became overcrowded.

Then his father gave him an old wooden box, with a lid,

which he said was a 'bible box', though there was nothing in it but a few cobwebs. Timmy swept these away and polished the box, inside and out, till it shone on the outside, and smelt of lavender inside. He lined it with a piece of blanket, partly covered by the black velvet.

Though the bone collection could not be classified like the stamps, or pressed and mounted and named like the flowers, Timmy spent a good deal of time arranging it and re-arranging it. His favourites shared a place on the black velvet. He enjoyed handling certain ones, stroking them and examining every curve, and occasionally licking them. They tasted of nothing except dryness, but their feel was more subtle. It had the smooth, slipperiness of a stick of chalk, and he almost expected – in vain – to see chalky marks left on his fingers.

One night, Timmy woke up suddenly. It was not the moon that woke him, as its beams had lain across his face for some time. It was a sound, or a combination of sounds. There was a distinct, dry rustling. Also a snuffling and snorting like some animal. Sometimes a subdued chinking of objects striking against each other; and the sensation of someone – or something – rootling or burrowing.

Worst of all, there was a dark shadow against the window, a shadow the size, and roughly the shape, of a person.

Timmy sat up. He was brave enough to do that, but by no means brave enough to get out of bed. The idea of his bare feet sharing the same floor as the unknown visitor's feet – if he or it *had* feet – terrified him. But with a sudden courage he did not suspect he possessed, he reached out a hand and switched on his bedside light.

'What are you doing in my room?' he asked, in rather a shaky voice.

The person, for it was a person, looked at him under shaggy

brows and grinned. He could see large, uneven, yellow teeth, with gaps here and there. He was dressed in a tattered uniform which Timmy recognized, from pictures, as being nautical. Something in the way the clothes clung to their wearer and the way the strands of hair hung dankly, suggested that the figure had just come out of water in which he had lain submerged for some time.

'I'm about my rightful business,' said the person. 'What are *you* doing, waking up in the middle of the night when all god-fearing children are asleep?'

'You woke me,' said Timmy, 'with your snufflings and snifflings and rustlings. Where do you come from?'

The thing scratched its head in bewilderment. 'I suppose if I said I'd come from Davy Jones's locker that would be about the size of it.'

'You mean you're really dead? Drowned and dead?'

'Yes, drowned and dead. But I can't rest peaceful in one place. I was restless all my life, roaming the seven seas, and now I'm dead, I can't rest either. I re-visit some of the places where I was most happy with my shipmates. Coral islands and golden sands and green valleys and gay little sea coast towns, where the girls were kind and the drink was strong.'

'It's not like that anywhere round here,' said Timmy firmly. 'No islands or golden sands. Or golden girls, either.'

'This is by nature of a business trip,' said the sailor. 'A mission, if you like. I'm not in search of treasure or loot. I only want my leg. I find I can't get on without it.'

Timmy's glance flew to the sailor's lower limbs. One was thin but unmistakably *there*, ending in a bare, brown, dirty foot, shod in a raffia sandal. But the other – well, the other was lacking. The trouser leg hung limply. This crippling depri-

vation necessitated the crutch that was tucked under the arm on that side. It was not a proper crutch, and looked as if it had been devised from a strong piece of driftwood.

'A man needs his rightful leg and it's no good to anyone else. I was just going through your box of bones. Some bonny bones you have here, to be sure. Now this here might be my leg.'

He snatched up the bone found in the cliff in Ireland and examined it carefully. To Timmy's horror, he raised it to his mouth and appeared to gnaw it, experimentally.

'It looks like mine. It feels like mine. It tastes like mine. I'd swear by all that's holy that it is mine. Now I shall be able to get around nimble-like, with no crutch to slow me down.'

'How did you happen to lose your leg?' asked Timmy.

'A shark bit it off below the knee when I was shipwrecked. A clean bite – a doctor couldn't have done it better. Now may I have this bone of yours, seeing that it's really mine? It's no use to you, is it?'

'Well, it is and it isn't. It happens to be my very favourite bone in my collection, that's all.'

'Well, it happens to be my very favourite leg, that's all. But I see your point. I'll bring you something in exchange when I'm next this way. It isn't only Davy Jones who has a locker. I've still got my old sea chest, down below. Goodbye, and thank 'ee very much. You're a brave lad. No one ever gave to the needy in vain.'

The sailor faded away into the moonlight, leaving the bible box open with the bones scattered untidily round.

I'll arrange them in the morning, thought Timmy, turning off the lamp and settling down in bed. But the darkness seemed to make a perfect background for his late visitor, crooked teeth and all, and he had to switch the light on again to banish the picture. This worked better and he was soon fast asleep.

'You must have been tired to go to sleep with your light on,' said his mother, when she came to wake him.

'I didn't. I mean I went to sleep once and then I woke up and couldn't get off again. So I turned my light on. It was a good idea because I did get off in the end.'

'Was it a bad dream that woke you?' said his mother, stroking his hair.

'Yes. No. I'm not sure. It seemed real.'

'Then it was a dream. They do seem real. Real as waking life.'

'And it was real,' thought Timmy as he dressed. 'Real as waking life. And so are my bones, all upset and messed about. And my best one gone.'

For several nights, nothing dramatic occurred. Timmy was apt to try and postpone going to bed, because getting off to sleep was so difficult. But as the nights went by, regular and uneventful, so his anticipation grew less. Just when he had almost ceased to expect his ghostly visitor from the sea, he re-appeared. Or Timmy supposed that was what had happened.

He slept very deeply that night after an extra long cross-country run at school, and it wasn't till he woke in the morning that he suspected he had been visited. As he lay in bed, he was aware of a salty, seaweedy yet mouldy smell. He jumped out of bed and there, on top of the bible box, was something he had always wanted – a ship in a bottle. She was a four-masted schooner, perfect in every detail, enclosed in a green glass bottle. She had *The Willing Lass* painted on the side.

Perhaps it was his ship, thought Timmy. His last ship. I suppose she is a wreck now.

He kept *The Willing Lass* long after the collection of bones had been turned out of the bible box to make room for a new collection of minerals. He kept it so long that it still stands on his mantelpiece now he is grown-up, and has a home of his own, and a little boy of his own who collects acorns. He has a hundred and seven, so far.

The Blood Stain

'There it is again,' said Rodney, reaching out an arm and prodding his brother Ted.

They were staying with their uncle and aunt, who lived in the country, and this was their first night away from home.

'What's the matter – leave me alone,' said Ted sleepily, turning over and huddling further under the bedclothes. But another, more energetic poke roused him.

'What did you say?'

'I said, there it is again. Listen! I've been hearing it off and on for ages.'

Ted's head emerged from under the blankets so that he could listen properly. Through the open window came a scrabbling sound, sometimes stopping for a few seconds, then starting again.

'It's an animal,' said Ted.

'Yes, that's what I think,' agreed Rodney.

'It's an animal digging. It's the Hound of the Baskervilles burying a bone.'

'A human one,' added Ted, with relish. They had read *The Hound of the Baskervilles* recently, and it had made a deep impression on them.

'I wish the thing would call it a day and stop,' said Rodney. 'It's just loud enough to keep me awake.'

'Me too, since you woke me. I might have slept through it but for you. Listen, it's stopped.'

They listened for a few minutes in silence.

'Thank goodness. Goodnight, Rod.'

'Goodnight, Ted. Oh, confound it, the creature has begun again.'

'It must be burying a whole skeleton.'

'Or digging up a whole skeleton.'

'Or maybe it's just digging for the hell of it. It may like digging holes.'

Gradually the noise subsided. The periods of silence got longer. The periods of activity shorter. Soon both boys were asleep.

Next morning, while they were having their breakfast, their uncle came into the room.

'Did you hear anything in the night?' he asked.

'Oh, I'd forgotten. Of course we did,' said Rodney. 'We heard a scraping, scrabbling kind of noise. We thought it was an animal digging.'

'A dog,' said Ted.

'Just come and have a look,' said their uncle.

'Let them finish their breakfast,' said their aunt. 'Whatever it is won't run away.'

'All right. Finish your food, lads, and then come into the front garden.'

The boys bolted their last slices of bread and marmalade and rushed into the small, walled garden which lay to the front of the cottage. Their uncle was standing near the corner of the wall, looking down into a deep, untidy hole.

'That's put paid to the lavender bush and my irises,' said their aunt, who had joined them. 'Vandalism, that's what I call it.'

'Vandalism it may be,' said their uncle, 'but it was a four-footed vandal by the look of things. What exactly did you hear, and when was it?' He turned to the boys.

'I've no idea of the time,' said Ted, 'but it was pretty dark and I'd been asleep for ages, or it felt like ages. Rod woke me, and then—'

'I'd been hearing the sound for about ten minutes,' said Rodney, and described what he had heard as well as he could.

'Was it a dog?' enquired Ted.

'Well, we haven't a dog and never have had. We're a cat family. If it was a dog, it must have been a fair size. There are no dogs very near here.'

'There's a couple of Corgies at the Hall,' said their aunt, 'but they'd never be loose at night. Proper pets they are.'

'No Corgi did that,' said their uncle. 'There's a terrier at the Post Office, but he's used as a watch-dog. A yapping little wretch he is, too. Always snapping at people.'

'There's a sheep-dog up at the farm, and an Alsatian at the garage. And that's about the lot. We're rather out of the village.' Their aunt looked sadly at her ruined plants.

'Have you any dogs who have been worrying sheep?' asked Ted, who was a town boy and got most of his knowledge of country ways from what he had read. 'I've heard of packs of wild dogs roaming over the countryside, savaging sheep and lambs.'

'Nothing like that round here, I'm glad to say. And what you described didn't sound as if there were a pack of dogs on the job. Do you think there could have been?'

'No, Uncle,' said both boys. 'There wasn't a bark or a snarl,' added Rodney. 'Surely there would have been if there had been more than one.'

'Of course there are other animals that dig holes,' said their aunt. 'Foxes and rabbits and badgers.'

'A rabbit couldn't have made such a big hole, and a fox or a badger would hardly have decided to make their earth so near human habitation, when there's all the countryside to

47

choose from. Well, whatever made it is going to have a disappointment if he comes back to finish the job. Fetch me my spade from the shed, Rodney. I'm going to fill up that hole.'

The spade was fetched and the hole filled up. Ginger, the house cat, spent much of the morning sniffing around the area and ended by digging several small holes himself. He had a liking for newly-disturbed soil.

The rest of the day passed quickly as there was so much to do. Their uncle let them have two old fishing rods and showed them how to use them. They spent hours by the stream, catching nothing but perfectly content. Only the biting midges drove them indoors at dusk.

'I wonder if we'll hear it again tonight,' said Ted, as they got ready for bed. 'Wake me if you hear anything.'

'You were annoyed when I woke you last night,' said Rodney.

'That was because I didn't know what I was being woken *for*. I want to be woken tonight.'

As it happened, both boys woke simultaneously when the scraping, scrabbling began again.

'Let's look out of the window. I don't think it's as dark as it was last night.'

'It's three o'clock,' said Ted, peering at his watch. 'The moon is shining – that's what makes the difference. Last night was cloudy.'

They jumped out of bed and drew back the curtains. There, in the angle of the stone wall, was the shape of a large dog, digging. The loose soil flew up between its back legs. It appeared to be pale grey or fawn in colour.

'Let's rap on the window.'

Neither of them felt inclined to go downstairs and out into the garden, where the mysterious hound was occupied with its nocturnal business.

THE BLOOD STAIN

'Yes. All right,' agreed Rodney. He knocked smartly on the pane with his knuckles. The sound had an instant effect on the lonely digger. He whipped round, raising his head to try and identify the noise. Then he leapt over the wall in a mighty bound and disappeared.

This time, the boys did not fall asleep so easily. They heard the dawn chorus – and then a distant cock crowing – while they discussed what they had seen. They both agreed that the creature was very large – a gigantic dog, and that it had terrific muscles as it sprang over the stone wall with one great leap, needing no preliminary run.

Next morning they slept late, and their aunt did not waken them. It was ten o'clock when they appeared downstairs for breakfast. Their uncle came in for an extra cup of tea, and sat down at the end of the table.

'Well, lads, what did you hear or see? There's another deep hole in the very same place, and we guessed you might have had a disturbed night. We heard nothing, sleeping round the back as we do. Now, out with it.'

Rodney and Ted, between them, related all they had seen and heard, and gave as complete a picture of the nocturnal visitor as was possible.

'You don't know what breed of dog?' asked their aunt.

'No,' said Rodney. 'We don't know many makes of dog, except the ordinary ones. This was a kind we'd never set eyes on before.'

'Uncle,' said Ted. 'Rod and me were talking about it in the night and we wondered if you'd mind letting us have a go.'

'Have a go at what?'

'At digging the hole a bit deeper. The dog must have been digging for something. Could we try to find out what it was, please?'

'He might have been going to bury something, not dig it up,' suggested their aunt.

'Oh, no, he wasn't,' said Rodney quickly. 'He would either have left it behind – in which case it would still be there. Or he took it off with him – then we should have seen it in his mouth when he turned and looked at the house, just before he jumped over the wall.'

'Dig away if you want,' said their uncle, 'as long as you put the soil back afterwards. I was thinking of laying a few

THE BLOOD STAIN

boulders over the place to discourage any further excavation. I still can, when you've finished.'

'Remember my plants,' begged their aunt. 'The border is thickly planted just there – such a sunny, sheltered corner. There's bergamot and sage and clove pinks.'

Having promised not to disturb a leaf, and to fill up the hole afterwards, the boys ate their breakfast hurriedly and set to work.

Digging was by no means as easy as they had imagined. The stones of the wall got in the way of their spades and they

resorted to a hand-fork and a trowel. If they came across a bulb they put it carefully on one side, to put back later.

'That dog must have sore paws,' said Ted, wiping his forehead with his sleeve. 'I think I'm beginning a blister.' He examined his palm critically.

'Is it worth going on?' asked Rodney. 'The hole's getting rather out of hand. The sides will be caving in if we're not careful.'

'Ought we to try to find some boards to shore it up?'

'We don't want to be a nuisance to uncle. He'd have to stop work and hunt around. He's sowing his winter lettuce in the vegetable plot.'

The clock in the sitting room chimed three-quarters.

'Getting on for twelve,' remarked Ted. 'Let's go on till it strikes twelve. Then we'll have a rest and start filling in.'

'And we can fish all the afternoon—'

'And after tea till supper—'

'Come on. One last effort.'

Just as the clock struck twelve, Rodney's trowel struck something unexpected. He let out a shout of triumph. Ted helped to clear away the earth to reveal a stout, wooden box, like a small chest, with iron bands round it. They worked carefully, frightened of damaging their find.

It was some time before they could raise the box from its resting place and stand it on the lawn. Ginger rubbed round their ankles, purring and arching his back.

'It's locked,' said Ted, trying to open the lid.

'We could force it, I think. But let's call uncle and aunt. It's really more theirs than ours.'

'But we found it,' said Rodney possessively. 'They'd never have taken the trouble. Still, I'll fetch them.' He ran off to find his uncle and his aunt appeared of her own accord, having heard their excited voices.

'Well, I never did. Who would have thought it!' she marvelled.

'It's a canny box,' said their uncle. 'Beautifully made.'

'How old is it?' asked Ted.

'That I can't say. A good age, I'd guess. It's many a long year since boxes were made like that, with those strong iron hinges and bands going round, and a set-in lock. Before my time.'

'Can we look inside?'

'We can and we will. Fetch me a screw-driver, one of you. In the drawer in the wash-house.'

Rodney ran off and returned with three screw-drivers of differing sizes. Their uncle selected one and began, very gently and cautiously, to raise the lid. It yielded gradually and revealed some white material inside. Or material that had once been white and was now yellowed with age.

'Handle it carefully. It may be rotten and dropping to pieces,' said their aunt. But it was still intact, though spotted with mildew.

'It's a kind of outer wrapping. This is the thing that's been so carefully preserved, folded inside.' He removed the outer covering and they saw the real treasure. Their aunt unfolded it with gentle fingers.

It was a robe for a baby, long and elaborate, with insets of fine lace and exquisitely embroidered.

'It looks too small for a baby,' said Ted, who knew very little about babies. 'It would fit a doll.'

'It's too pretty for a doll,' said Rodney, who knew even less about dolls.

'It's just right for a baby,' said their aunt. 'Just right. Babies used to wear long clothes when they were very young. I've a photograph of my own mother, being held by her mother, wearing just such a robe. But it's very grand for every day use. It may have been a christening robe. Perhaps an heirloom that was handed on from one generation to the next. That's what it will be.'

'You don't think it was a shroud?' said their uncle. 'It seems more reasonable to find a shroud buried deep in the ground.'

'But where's the baby?' asked Rodney. 'An empty shroud seems rather pointless.'

'I'm jolly glad it is empty,' said Ted.

'So am I,' agreed his aunt. 'Very glad indeed. There must be some story behind this that we may never know.'

'Are we going to bury it again?'

'Oh no, Rod. We'll keep it and I'll wash it and there's a chance that some antiquarian could tell us a little more. Or someone at a museum.'

'Help me to fill in the hole, lads. Then we'll put some tidy-sized boulders on the top. Our midnight hound will have his work cut out if he tries to move them. He'll need paws of iron, not flesh and blood.'

'I bet his paws aren't flesh and blood,' whispered Ted to Rodney.

The three of them filled in the hole and put four great stones on the top. Then they replanted the few bulbs they had displaced, and it was time for dinner. Afterwards they fished happily till tea, and again till the midges drove them indoors.

After supper, their aunt spread the little robe out on the table to look at at leisure. She examined some of the stitching with a magnifying glass.

'It's exquisite,' she said. 'All hand-done, of course. I've never seen such fine work in my life. Have a look for yourself.' She handed the magnifying glass to Rodney.

'I say, Ted, come and have a dekko. This embroidery on

THE BLOOD STAIN

the skirt isn't just fancy stitching, it's a sort of picture. I can see a peacock with his tail outspread. And two crossed keys.'

'So can I,' agreed Ted. And their aunt saw the same.

'What patience!' she sighed. 'Every feather in the tail perfect, and the close feathers on the breast, too. Couldn't have done her eyesight much good, whoever did it. I hope she worked in a good light. I'll wash it in the morning, if it's a good drying day. I don't suppose the spots of mildew will come out, but I hope this large, nasty brown stain will.'

There was a brown mark on the skirt, the only real blemish.

'Do you think it's blood?' suggested Rodney.

'What a disagreeable idea – but you might be right. I'll soak that part in salt water over night and see if it comes out.'

'It's blood,' repeated Rodney, confidently. 'You know how often criminals are given away because of old blood stains. They must be hard to get rid of or the criminals would have got rid of them. Or that's what happens in books.'

The night was peaceful and nothing disturbed the boys' sleep. In the morning the stones were in position on top, just as they had been left. Ginger was curled up asleep on the flattest one, with his furry cheek resting on a ginger paw. It was a warm, sunny morning with a gentle breeze.

Soaking and washing and bleaching in the sun, and very careful pressing, improved the little garment, but the brown stain lingered on.

Rodney and Ted were much more anxious than their uncle and aunt to find out more about the mysterious box and its contents. The grown-ups treated the discovery as something quite inexplicable, but were resigned to leave it that way. Their attitude infuriated the boys.

'We shall have to do something if they won't,' said Rodney.

'But what? We've only another ten days before we go back home.'

'Ten days ought to be plenty. Have you any ideas, Ted.'

'No, none. How could I have?'

'Well, one of us had better come up with an idea jolly quick. Think. Think hard. Use your little grey cells, as Poirot advises. Great crimes are often solved without the detective moving from his armchair.'

'Like Sherlock Holmes?' suggested Ted.

'Yes, like Sherlock Holmes. We'll have to begin by finding out if Uncle or Auntie knows anything that might help. They've lived here all their lives.'

'Auntie,' said Rodney, during dinner, 'are there any of the people you mentioned – antiquires or something – living round here?'

'Oh, you mean antiquarians. Yes, there's one, she's a comparative newcomer. She lives at Mill Cottage and her name is Mrs Rennie.'

'What does she do?'

'She looks after her house and garden like the rest of us,' said his aunt. 'But she writes books in her spare time. She's written one about the church.'

'Proper upset she was,' went on their uncle, 'when she found the old pew ends had been burned. All wormy they were and falling to pieces. But she would have it they were unique and should have been preserved.'

'Could we show her the robe?' asked Ted.

'You could if you had a mind. She likes children and is always filling the cottage with noisy grandchildren. Wild as gipsies, they are.'

That afternoon, the boys set out for Mill Cottage with the robe, carefully packed by their aunt, in a plastic carrier. They found Mrs Rennie at the top of a step-ladder, painting the kitchen ceiling yellow. When she heard they had a problem, she descended rapidly, and they went into the garden with a mug of coffee for her and cokes for themselves.

Mrs Rennie was certainly used to children and it was not difficult to persuade Rodney and Ted to tell their story. Indeed, it would have been more difficult to stop them. She listened without interrupting once. When they had told all, there was a pause. She examined the robe carefully and used the magnifying glass they had brought with them. Her serious expression never wavered.

'There's one thing I can tell you straight away. The peacock with the spread tail and the crossed keys were the crest of the Derwent family, who lived at the Old Hall in the village from the time of the Stuarts till the early nineteenth century. There were some Latin words associated with the crest which mean, roughly: Cross Keys. Cross my heart. Never fail. The little robe must be something to do with them. It's so fine and costly and beautiful that it must almost certainly have been an heirloom. Possibly kept for the christening of the eldest son and heir.'

'But the box? And the great dog? Where do they fit in?' asked Ted.

'And the blood stain,' added Rodney.

'That I can't tell you. But I go to London every Wednesday to work at the British Museum or the Record Office, and I'll look up a few records. That's tomorrow, you know. Try to cheer up. Perhaps I shall be lucky and light on something relevant. You never can tell.'

'We've learned something,' said Rodney, as they walked back. 'It was to do with the Derwents.'

They related all they had found out to their uncle and aunt, who were familiar with the name Derwent.

'Their tombs are all over the church,' said their aunt. 'I used to have a good look at one of them, when I was a little girl and the sermon was boring. Sermons were much longer in those days. The writing said:

LORD DAVID DERWENT
Died 1777

I remember it because of all the sevens.'

The next evening, the boys were eager to go round to Mill Cottage, but their aunt wouldn't allow them. 'She'll be worn out, poor lady. Let her be till tomorrow. She goes off by the seven o'clock bus, I've heard, to catch the train at the junction.' But Mrs Rennie did not let them down. She arrived after supper bearing news that would not wait.

'By the greatest good luck in the world, I've found some links in the chain,' she said. 'There's a legend – I'm afraid it

THE BLOOD STAIN

isn't an historical fact, but it's a legend – about a little Lady Lavinia Derwent who mysteriously disappeared from her cradle. And the faithful hound who always watched over her disappeared too. Never a trace of her was found, and the dog never re-appeared either.'

'But why the box?'

'Why the robe?'

'Where did the dog come from that *we* saw?'

'How did the christening robe come to be buried in the box?'

'What about the blood stain—'

'That won't wash away?'

Mrs Rennie got up and shook hands with the grown-ups.

'It's a wonderful find,' she said. 'Simply wonderful. I advise you to take it to a costume expert at a museum who should be able to date it. As for you two—' she smiled warmly at the boys. 'You'll just have to answer your questions yourselves. Your guess is as good as mine – or better. Come and see me again, one day.'

She strode off into the evening.

Twin Stars

Rachel and Fay were born in the same year, on the same day, and even the same hour, at the same Maternity Clinic. They were twins by accident, and here the likeness began and ended – or so it seemed. Rachel was thin and dark, with a head of black curls. Fay was plump and rosy, with long, straight, golden hair.

Their mothers, Mrs Pine and Mrs Whitney, remained friends after meeting in hospital. They saw each other again, pushing prams in the park, and later on at nursery school, and later still at 'big school'. They even attempted a joint birthday party, which was such a success that it was repeated in the years that followed.

'We were born under the same star,' said Rachel to Fay, one day, having just discovered the existence of astrology.

'What does that mean exactly?' asked Fay.

'I don't know *exactly* but lots of clever people who study the stars can find out what kind of a person you are going to be, if they know the exact time of your birth. As we were born at the same time, we must be the same kind of girls.'

'We couldn't look more different, could we? I'm so horribly fat and moon-faced with hair straight as straight, and you are so gorgeously thin and pale, with hair that will never need a perm.'

'I don't think we need look alike on the outside,' said Rachel thoughtfully. 'It's only the inside that matters.'

'We get on well, anyhow. You're my very best friend and always will be.'

They smiled at each other.

Rachel and Fay were nice, ordinary children, neither brilliant nor stupid, and in no way remarkable except to their parents. The other girls liked them reasonably well, though they were neither of them popular enough to be voted Form Captain. Nor would they have enjoyed this honour as they were naturally shy and avoided the limelight when possible.

But if on-lookers had observed them more carefully, several interesting points would have emerged. They did not only share activities when together, which was natural; they seemed to be aware of each other in absence, too.

When the games mistress asked Rachel, reading in the library, where Fay was, Rachel had no hesitation in replying: 'She's playing tennis on the end court,' though Rachel had never stirred from her chair and could not possibly have *seen* which court Fay had found free.

Similarly, when Rachel was late for school and Fay was asked if she knew the reason, Fay explained that Rachel had dashed back home to fetch a book she had forgotten. This sounded plausible enough, and was proved to be true when Rachel arrived a few minutes later, pink in the face and breathless, with her Latin book under her arm.

What no one knew, neither staff nor girls, was that Rachel and Fay had not previously set eyes on each other that morning, as they lived in opposite directions and Rachel had not missed the book till she was half-way to school.

They never discussed this special understanding they shared as they had experienced it all their lives, and it was as natural as breathing. If Fay appeared at a maths lesson without her compass, Rachel reminded her that she had left it in her bedroom the night before, when she'd taken her book up to bed in a last, vain attempt to solve a problem. It was still on her bedside table.

'So it is,' agreed Fay. 'Now I remember.'

Sometimes there was an incident that drew the attention – and often the teasing – of the rest of the class. One day, Rachel came to school with her hair tied in bunches, and the same morning Fay turned up with her long, pale hair tied in two bunches as well.

'We all know you are twins, or kind of twins,' said one critic, 'but there's no need to carry it too far. It's all right Fay doing her hair this way, but yours looks frightful, Rachel.'

'No, Rachel's is super but Fay's is a mess.'

When Rachel and Fay declared they hadn't planned to change their hair styles together, the other girls just laughed.

'Sez you,' someone retorted.

'There's no need to tell lies about it – who cares how you do your hair?'

Rachel and Fay exchanged unhappy glances. They didn't know why they'd had the same idea the same morning. But it was a fact. They were glad when the bell rang for assembly.

Then things took a more serious turn. There was the never to be forgotten day when the headmistress sent for them. They stood in her room, blushing and uncomfortable, though neither could think of anything she had done wrong.

'The similarity between your history examination papers is too marked to be coincidence,' said Miss Feather, gravely. 'One of you must have copied from the other. Have you anything to say?'

'No, Miss Feather.'

'No, Miss Feather.'

'I should like you to think again. I know you are close

TWIN STARS

friends and have been so ever since you came to this school. I don't doubt that either of you would gladly help the other when in trouble. But such help in examinations is a luxury you cannot allow yourselves. It is not fair to the other girls in the class, and in the long run it is not fair to yourselves. Examinations are the best method so far devised of testing what each candidate has learned. You understand me?'

'Yes, Miss Feather. I didn't help Fay. She wouldn't have let me.'

'And I didn't copy from Rachel. I wouldn't have dreamed of copying from anybody. Besides, I didn't need to. I found the paper easy.'

'And so did I.'

Miss Feather paused, with a puzzled expression on her thin, kindly face.

'Have you anything more to say, Fay?'

'No, Miss Feather.'

'Or you, Rachel?'

'No, Miss Feather.'

'I'm disappointed with one of you, but I don't know which.' For the first time, she allowed herself to smile wryly.

'Please think seriously about what has happened. Don't be too upset – it's not the end of the world. And it's not the end of the close, warm friendship between you which I hope will last for many years. You may go.'

'Thank you, Miss Feather.'

'Thank you.'

'I shall not bring up the subject again unless your future conduct forces me to do so. And no one else will mention it either.'

But alas, this was not so. For the rest of the examination period, they were moved to seats far apart. The other girls both noticed and commented.

'I thought your history marks were suspicious,' said one girl, '82 and 81.'

'Who found you out? Did Miss Price (their form mistress) tell tales?'

'So that was the reason for your mysterious summons to the Feather. Was she fierce? Did she say she was "surprised and pained" – that's her pet phrase.'

'Some schools expel people who cheat.'

'You mean people who are *found* cheating!'

'It wasn't like that at all,' said Fay, stung to retort. 'You don't know what you're talking about. You know nothing at all, so you'd better keep quiet.'

'As if we would cheat,' said Rachel. 'You're disgusting with your insinuations.'

'And I suppose Miss Price was unfair to move Rachel into the back row?' taunted someone.

'She just doesn't understand—' protested Rachel, who liked and admired her form mistress.

No one in the school, neither staff nor girls, dared say a word openly, when the maths marks were put up. Rachel and Fay tied in the sixth place with 65 per cent.

'It's a good thing you were moved,' said Fay to Rachel. 'That will show them.'

But what precisely it would show them, neither girl knew. They had the same marks in maths. Yes, it would show that, particularly notable as this mark was based on the result of three papers, arithmetic, geometry and algebra. But would it reveal something else? Some bond between them which was there, though unrecognized.

'When I'm older,' said Fay suddenly. 'I shall have my horoscope cast. Someone said it costs £5.'

'So shall I. When I get £5. I know Daddy would never pay for me to have it cast now. He says it's all rubbish and a waste of money. He and Mummy laugh at the forecasts in the local paper, the bit headed: *What the Stars Say*.'

'My mother says only superstitious, uneducated people believe in forecasts. Do you ever read them?'

'Yes,' said Rachel. 'Nearly always.'

'So do I. But what do you think of them?'

'They don't seem to apply. I don't think they are meant for children. The other week mine – well ours – said I was going on a long journey over the sea, soon. It's very unlikely till the summer holidays and it's only December, now. Even then we shall probably only go to the coast. That's about two hours in the car.'

'I feel the same,' said Fay, sympathetically. 'Once it said I'd come in for a large sum of money. Children don't usually come in for large sums of money. I don't think they're allowed to go in for the pools.'

'We'll have to wait till we're grown-up. Then our forecasts may make more sense.'

'Yes, we'll have to wait. I wonder if they'll be exactly the same? The horoscopes, I mean.'

'We'll have to find out the exact moment of our birth. There may have been a few minutes between.'

'Perhaps the hospital keeps accurate records.'

'If we were born the same minute, does it mean we'll have the same fate? The same career and the same number of children?'

'Then we'll have to marry the same man!' said Fay.

'He'll have to be a Mormon!' added Rachel.

The conversation ended in helpless giggles.

When the summer holidays came, Rachel, as expected, went to the sea for a fortnight with her family. They usually went to the same little place, but this year there was a slight variation in their programme. Rachel and her brother, Jim, took their bicycles. This meant that they were more independent than on previous holidays. They could cycle to the next town, or go inland to picnic spots by the quiet, gliding river, with its flowery banks and water meadows dotted with cows.

Rachel and Fay had become very keen cyclists and were longing for the day when they could go Youth Hostelling on their bicycles. Jim was single-minded, too, and had only one idea – always the same. That idea was fishing. Fortunately the places thought good for fishing suited Rachel almost as well. She lay in the long grass reading her book, or gathered flowers, or wrote lengthy letters to Fay, at home.

'Are you writing to Fay again?' asked Jim, as he settled himself and his gear on the bank, and made what he considered to be a perfect cast.

'Yes, I am. Why not?'

'But you wrote yesterday. Nothing has happened since then.'

'It was the day before, actually, when we were picnicking by the mill race. Lots has happened since then. Or I've lots to say, which is all that matters. And letters are boring if they are all news, like a newspaper.'

'Oh you girls! Waffle – waffle – waffle – pages and pages of waffle. There's nothing I want to say to my friends that won't go on a postcard. Even on a picture postcard.'

'True enough,' agreed Rachel. 'I could write one for you. Shall I? – "Am having a great time. The weather is great. The fishing is great. I caught a trout nine inches long. Yours Jim".'

'Fair enough,' said Jim good humouredly. 'But the length of the trout was underestimated. It was nine-and-a-half inches long. You've no regard for accuracy.'

Rachel went on with her letter and Jim went on with his fishing. The pair of them got on together extremely well, though this might not be obvious to an outsider, who only heard them arguing.

Fay, left at home, missed Rachel badly, especially as her little sister was five years younger than herself, and not allowed to go on long bicycle rides. But the fortnight went slowly by, with the interest of Rachel's long letters, to which she replied at equal length. She also went on bicycle rides by herself.

One day, she planned to ride five miles to the next town, to buy a paperback she wanted to read, which was unobtainable at the local newsagent. It was a life of Lady Jane Grey, who was one of her heroines, just then. So young – so learned – such an unspeakably tragic figure. Rachel and she often talked about her. She would have finished the book before

Rachel's return and then she would lend it to her. Two days would be ample time. Fay swallowed books as a starving person swallowed a crumb.

Fay took the main road, which was uncomfortably crowded with holiday traffic, and successfully purchased her book. It had a very moving cover, showing Lady Jane, a miracle of youth and sadness, standing under the oaks at Bradgate Park. The old man with his hand on her shoulder, was no doubt her beloved tutor, Roger Ascham. Fay treated herself to an ice-cream and read the first few pages while she ate it. It started well and she longed to read on, but her father had spoken to her only that morning about being late for meals and causing extra work. So she closed the book reluctantly, tucked it into her bicycle basket, and started for home.

She decided to take another route, as the main road had been so noisy and crowded. There was a back way, about a mile longer, which was quieter. This would be more pleasant. When she had gone half-way, and was approaching a very steep hill, she felt an ominous grating and bumping. A flat tyre. She dismounted and investigated. Her back tyre was flat. She pumped it up, but she could hear the air escaping when she stopped. There was nothing for it but to walk. It was only another two miles. Still, it was a pity she would be late for dinner when she had organized her morning in order to be punctual.

The road was deserted and she thought she might manage to read her book as she pushed her bicycle. She opened it, rested it on the handlebars, and tried, but it was not a success. The steering became erratic as she was using only one hand, and the book kept slipping. She closed it regretfully, just as a large lorry thundered by, taking up most of the lane and driving her into the hedge.

'Shouldn't be allowed on this narrow lane,' she thought, echoing her father.

A few minutes later, the lane was alive with speeding vehicles. First a police car, sounding its siren. Then an ambulance, followed by several more police cars. Fay flattened herself against the bank, watching them flash past, her heart beating quickly. The wail of the sirens filled her with panic.

There must have been an accident, a major one, on Gallow's Hill. She would have to pass it. She hoped no one was killed. She shrank from the picture of death and destruction, and broken bodies laid by the roadside with their faces covered.

The reality, when she caught up with it, was even more terrifying. She came to police notices of ACCIDENT, flashing lights, and a notice saying: STOP. There, blocking most of the lane, was the lorry. It had mounted the bank, ploughing a great gash as it went, and then overturned. Damage on either side of the lane showed that it had lurched from side to side on its headlong career. Traffic was stopped in both directions. A kindly policeman beckoned her on, and pushed her bicycle for her along the narrow strip of the road that was left free.

'I had a puncture and that's why I'm walking,' said Fay.

'Thank God for that,' said the policeman. 'You might have been killed if you'd been on the hill on your bicycle. The lorry got out of control – it should never have been allowed in this country lane, anyhow, and it careered down, crashing from side to side. Now just go on quietly and be thankful.'

'The driver?'

'Oh, he's dead and his mate is terribly injured.'

Feeling rather shaky and sick, Fay continued on her way. When she had related her adventure to her mother, and been kissed and hugged, and eaten her hot meal, she felt better.

She settled down in the garden, not to read the tempting *Lady Jane Grey*, but to compose a long letter to Rachel. It would be the last time she would be able to write, as Rachel would be home in two days. Her narrow escape lost nothing in the telling, and when she had finished the letter, she felt much more cheerful.

When Rachel arrived back, she unpacked hastily, but only because requested to do so by her mother, and set out on her bicycle to visit Fay. The pair went into the garden, to sit in the swing-seat and recount any news that had been omitted from their lengthy epistles. It was soon clear that Rachel had something to tell of the utmost importance. Fay lay back to listen.

'Thank you for your last letter,' said Rachel. 'I got it yesterday. You know, the one where you narrowly escaped death.'

'Yes, I know,' said Fay, 'but it may not have been as narrow as all *that*. It's difficult to work out times and speeds. Though even Daddy agreed with the policeman that I was probably very lucky.'

'Something happened to me that morning, too,' went on Rachel. 'Not dramatic like you, but uncanny all the same.'

'You mean like the other queer things that have happened?'

'Yes. In a way. Anyhow, I'll tell you. Jimmy was going fishing in the Mill pond and I cycled there with him – it's about three miles. I meant to stay with him as usual, but I found I was bored. We'd been there before, and I finished my book and had forgotten to bring another. I hadn't any paper to write to you on, and I got two frightful horse-fly bites. That's how I got this huge lump on my forehead. Anyhow, when it got to about twelve, I decided to go back alone. I told Jimmy he could eat my share of the picnic, except my bar of chocolate, and I set out.

'I'd got about half-way, when I suddenly felt I *must* get off my bicycle, and walk.'

'Was something wrong?' asked Fay.

'Nothing at all. The bike was in perfect order. I just felt I must get off. I can't explain why. So I did. And I walked home.'

'Didn't you feel silly, pushing your bike for no reason?'

'Not really, or not then. I knew I had to. It made me late back to the boarding house. I did undo the valve in my back tyre when I got near the village, and let out the air. Then I should have a perfectly good explanation if anyone asked me why I was walking.'

'And did they?'

'No, they didn't. I just had to pump up my tyre afterwards. I joined mummy and daddy on the beach and finished off their picnic. They didn't ask any awkward questions. Mummy fussed a bit over my horse-fly bites which were swelling up. It all seemed queer, and when I read your letter it seemed queerer still. I must have started walking just about the time you had your puncture.'

'The same day—' said Fay.

'The same hour—' added Rachel.

'The same minute—' they said together.

This was some years ago. Rachel and Fay are still friends and have been Youth Hostelling together all over the east of England. Now they are at the same university, both reading history. But their boy friends are quite different. Rachel's is a rock-climber and a rugger player. Fay's dislikes games and hopes to be a poet. They haven't had their horoscopes cast yet. It seems less important now they are older, and so much is happening.

Rock-a-bye-baby

'What are you doing, mother?' asked Laurel, anxiously. She was four years old and easily frightened. Her mother often told her she was scared of her own shadow. That morning, her mother had pulled down the ladder that led up to the roof, and had gone up the steps. Laurel could hear muffled bumps and thumps and the rustling of paper.

'What are you doing?' she repeated.

Her mother's face appeared in the opening made by the trap door. She had a smear of dirt across her cheek and her hair was untidy, two unusual things. Laurel thought she did not look like her own mother at all. She looked strange. And her voice echoed in a queer way too. She called down:

'Just getting something I wanted out of the roof. I hadn't realized how dirty everything gets if it's neglected. I haven't been up here for ages.'

'Not since you got the big suitcase down,' said Laurel. 'I came to look too and it was horrid. Horrid! Horrid!'

'Yes, I remember. You cried because something frightened you. But it doesn't take much to frighten you, does it?'

'It was the cobwebs,' said Laurel, 'those clinging, sticky cobwebs. And that spider who made a noise with his feet when he walked.'

'But you love spiders in the garden, don't you?'

'They're different. They're clean and quiet and have

crosses on their backs like little hot cross buns. Oh, what's that thing you're holding – is it a box?'

'No, it isn't. I'll show you when I've brought it down. It's rather heavy. Perhaps I ought to have waited till your father came home. But I wanted it cleaned up as a surprise. Stand out of the way. I'll manage if I take it slowly.'

Laurel stood well out of the way and watched her mother negotiating something heavy down the ladder, something loosely wrapped in a piece of material. Then, as it landed on the carpet below, she saw exactly what it was, even before it was uncovered.

'Why, it's a cradle! A lovely old wooden cradle like the picture in my *Mother Goose* book of "Hush-a-bye-baby".'

'Help me to take the wrappings off. It's a tattered old bedspread. There. We'll put it on the kitchen table and have a good look at it.'

'May I get in it, mother, and rock? Please may I get in it?'

'Wait till it's clean and nice. Let's just look at it first.'

The cradle was enchanting, with wooden rockers and a wooden hood at one end. It had a band of carving on each side and a date carved on top of the hood – 1773.

First her mother brushed it thoroughly. Then wiped it well with a damp cloth. Laurel was surprised to see how quickly the cloth became black. Then, when the wood was dry, she helped her mother to polish it with lavender polish. Her mother rubbed the polish on, being careful to get into the cracks and crannies of the carving. Laurel, supplied with a yellow duster, helped to rub it off. After they had worked for some time and Laurel's arms were aching, the wood shone and the cradle looked – and smelt – attractive.

Laurel climbed inside and curled up.

'How deep it is. Did I have lots of blankets under me so I could see out?'

ROCK-A-BYE-BABY

'You were never in the cradle till this minute,' said her mother. 'Neither was I.'

Laurel's face fell. She could almost remember being in the cradle.

'You needn't cry about it,' said her mother cheerfully.

'Didn't I have a cradle?' wailed Laurel.

'You had a carricot, which was more convenient. You must have seen other babies in them. They have handles and can easily be carried about, and put on the back seat of a car.'

'The baby who slept in this cradle couldn't have been carried about in it much,' said Laurel. 'I suppose her mother carried her about in her arms everywhere. That would be best. I wish I'd been that baby.' She sighed.

'The baby who first used that cradle was born over two hundred years ago. 1773.'

'Who was the first baby?'

'I don't know. It belonged to someone in your father's family. When Granny McFie died two years ago, her treasures were shared out between Uncle Angus and Aunty Jean and your father. And the cradle came to your father.'

'How lucky that he got this lovely cradle. Didn't he sleep in it?'

'No. The family moved about a great deal and the cradle was forgotten. Your father had something much more convenient.'

The cradle stood in the sitting room, in the bay window, and everyone who came to the house admired it. Laurel often got inside and rocked herself, and traced the carving with an exploring finger. Sometimes she laid her doll Phoebe in it and sang to her. She sang 'Hush-a-bye-baby' and 'Golden slumbers'.

Soon after the cradle had been brought down from the roof, Laurel woke up in the middle of the night. This was nothing new. As she grew older, these wakings became more distressing, rather than less. First, she always made sure she was in her own bed, with Phoebe by her side. Then she stretched out an arm to feel her clothes lying tidily on her chair. Then, as she tried to settle again for sleep, came those mysterious whisperings and rustlings that filled her with terror. Those muffled voices and stealthy footsteps which turned the daytime house into a place of dread and despair. Her heart beat quicker – her palms were damp with

ROCK-A-BYE-BABY

perspiration – her throat was constricted. She bore it as long as she could, then she had to cry out; 'Mother! Mother! Mother!' The words echoed through the sleeping house.

Her mother came at once, tall and remote in her long nightgown, her dark hair tied back. A cool hand was laid on her forehead:

'There's nothing wrong, Laurel. You're in your own bed with Mother and Father just through the wall. You're too big to wake us all just because *you* happen to be awake. People often lie awake in the night, for hours and hours.'

'But not little children—'

'Yes, some little children lie awake, too. But they know they can come to no harm in their own homes. They say poems and tell themselves stories till they drop off again. They don't wake their parents.'

'Some do,' muttered Laurel.

'Then some children are selfish. Now, I'll get you a drink of water and turn your pillow over. That will be better. Gracious, your forehead is all wet. I'll get a tissue.'

But the moment of parting came all too soon. The cool kiss – the firm tucking up – then the closing of the door.

'Mother, let me come into your bed. Please let me come! I'll be as still as a mouse.'

'No, Laurel, you must stay in your own bed. Your father works hard at the garage and he needs a good night's sleep. You mean to lie still, I know, but you wriggle like an eel. No one else can sleep a wink. Goodnight. Think of something pleasant and you'll soon be asleep. Then it will be morning and you'll hear the birds singing.'

Laurel tried to think of something pleasant. She thought of the slide in the park and the rush of air as she sped down. But what had happened? The slide had no end. She went faster and faster – she couldn't stop. Something horrible waited for her at the bottom, something with long black legs like a spider in the roof. She must call out. She must! She must!

'Mother! Mother!' rang through the house once more.

But this particular time when she woke, there were no disturbing voices or footsteps, whether under the bed or on the stairs. There was just one clear, unmistakable sound. It was a baby crying.

Laurel was too young to question the evidence of her senses. There was a baby crying. Whose baby, she did not know. Where it was she did not know either. But it was certainly a baby. And a very unhappy baby, too. Although she was surprised to hear a baby, she was not terrified as she had been by the previous mumblings and shufflings. She knew quite well that a baby could not harm her. It couldn't walk – perhaps it couldn't even sit up – it could only cry. But where could the baby have come from? While pondering this problem, she drifted off to sleep.

'I didn't call you in the night,' she told her mother proudly the next morning, as her mother brushed her dark hair.

'Did you want to?'

'Well, I nearly did. There was a baby crying somewhere and it kept me awake. But I wasn't really frightened. It couldn't *do* anything to me. It was only a baby. And a very little baby.'

'Then you must have been dreaming. There's no baby in this house or next door. But even if it was a dream, you were a good girl not to call me. A good, brave girl.' Her mother gave her a kiss on the back of her neck.

The next night she heard the baby again. And the night after that. And the following one. She knew she was wide awake and that it wasn't a dream, but she did not know how to convince her mother that this was so. Each time the crying stopped suddenly.

'Why do babies cry?' she inquired the next day.

'Oh, because they're hungry or cold, or just to exercise their lungs. Or they might have wind.'

'What's wind? Did I have it?'

'All babies have it sometimes. It's a pain in their tummies. You hold them up against your shoulder and pat their back. Then they give a hiccup and feel better.'

On the next night, the crying was louder than ever. The baby sounded in pain. Its wails went up and down in a persistent rhythm. Laurel found it quite impossible to get off to sleep. She was not frightened of the baby, but she was in mortal fear of the dark. Particularly the darkness that filled the landing and spilled down the stairs into the hall. Supposing she couldn't find the switch? Once out of bed she felt vulnerable. Supposing she trod on something? Something that was not there in the daylight? Or supposing something reached out a skinny hand and gripped her ankle? There were endless possibilities.

But the crying went on. Laurel gathered together what courage she could muster. She took the warm, knitted quilt off Phoebe's cot and opened the bedroom door. To her surprise and relief, moonlight streamed through the staircase window, lighting up each step. She crept downstairs, crossed the hall, and opened the sitting room door. There stood the cradle by the window, silvery in the moonlight. She stood still and stared. The cradle was gently rocking, all by itself. Gently, but unmistakably.

She went on watching. The rocking was slight, but there could be no mistake. As she stood, spell bound, she saw a tiny hand flapping, a hand not much bigger than Phoebe's. This tiny hand, with its appeal for help, strengthened her

determination and her shaking legs, though even then it was several minutes before she crossed the carpet and looked inside the cradle.

There, deep down, lay a tiny baby in a long white robe, with a lace cap on its little head. Its face was red and its minute fists were purple and mottled. They were tightly clenched.

'There, my darling,' whispered Laurel. 'I'll snuggle you up. You'll soon be warm and comfy.' She tucked Phoebe's quilt cosily over the infant. The crying stopped like magic and the angry red face uncrumpled, as she put the little hands under the coverlet.

'I'm glad it wasn't wind,' thought Laurel thankfully. 'I'm

not sure I would have dared hold her against my shoulder and pat her back till she hiccuped.'

Just as she was leaving the cradle, which was now motionless, she saw something gleaming near the baby's head. It was a little, silver bell. She took it back to bed with her, feeling, in a muddled way, that the bell would show she was speaking the truth. Everyone would have to believe her when they saw it. It was proof.

Laurel fell asleep as quickly as the baby in the cradle, and she did not wake till her mother drew back the curtains.

'I heard the baby crying again last night,' she said. 'Louder than ever. And I went downstairs in the moonlight and covered the cradle with Phoebe's warm, knitted cover. Then it was quiet and went to sleep. It's little hands were purple with cold. And I found this in the cradle – in your cradle.' She took the silver bell from under her pillow.

'How brave of you, darling,' said her mother, 'to go downstairs all alone. How very brave. I'm proud of you.' She gave Laurel an unexpectedly warm, close hug and kissed her all over her face. Even the tip of her nose, in a way that Laurel loved.

They went downstairs hand in hand, and looked in the cradle together. There was Phoebe's knitted cover, but nothing else.

That evening, Laurel's father unlocked the safe and brought out something wrapped in a piece of silk. It was a baby's rattle, with a handle of mother-of-pearl and five silver bells.

'You see?' said her mother. 'There were once six. This is where the sixth one hung. It exactly matches the others.'

Her father examined the odd bell found in the cradle and agreed. 'We'll have it put back by a jeweller,' he said, 'if I can't manage it myself.'

'I've never seen this before,' said Laurel, taking the rattle in her hand and jingling the bells. 'Where did it come from?'

'Your Granny McFie gave it to me when father and I got married, seven years ago. It was an heirloom. She wanted me to have it because I'd married the eldest son.'

'Did I jingle it when I was a baby?'

'Yes, you did. You loved it. And you used to bite the silver ring when you were cutting your teeth.'

'Why did you put it away? I still like it.'

'I put it away because I wanted to keep it very safe. It's real silver and very old. So I asked father to lock it in the safe till it was wanted again.'

'Who was the baby who rattled it first? Was it you?' She looked at her father inquiringly.

'Oh no, though I used to have it. It goes back several generations, perhaps to your great-great-great grandfather.'

'Babies used to wear funny little caps then. I know, because the baby who was crying had one. When will the rattle be wanted again?'

'This autumn,' said her mother. 'I'm having another baby in October.'

'Will it be a girl or a boy?'

'I shan't know till it arrives. Which would you prefer, a sister or a brother?'

'I don't mind. Perhaps a boy. No perhaps a girl. Couldn't it be twins?'

When October came, John Phillip was born, and slept peacefully in the wooden cradle, but he had a carricot as well, for when he went visiting. He was a contented little person and hardly cried at all. He soon learned to wave his rattle and jingle the bells.

Laurel could do almost everything for him, even get his wind up. She often kissed his little fists as they reminded her so vividly of the ghost baby in the moonlit cradle. But John Phillip's were warm, not cold.

When she was older, and John Phillip was running about, Laurel asked her mother something that had been on her mind for some time. It was much easier to ask her mother things nowadays. Life was easier all round. She hardly ever woke in the night and felt sure she would never hear the baby cry again.

'Mother, the baby I saw in the cradle that night must have been a ghost. And she must have been the ghost of someone. Who was it? I'd like to know. I often think of her.'

Her mother hesitated before answering.

'A sad thing happened over a hundred years ago,' she said at last. 'A little, new-born baby girl was asleep there and a cat jumped into the cradle and went to sleep on her face. She couldn't breathe. She was suffocated.'

'Did it – was it – I mean, did she know what was happening?'

'No, darling. She just fell more deeply asleep and never woke.'

'So that's why you won't let me have a kitten?'

'It is, partly. But you can have a kitten when John Phillip is bigger. Perhaps when he's four. Then he'll be old enough to be gentle with it.'

'Pussy cat now!' shouted John Phillip. 'I want a pussy cat now.'

'Meow! Meow!' said Laurel, prancing about on all fours. 'Let's both be pussy cats. Meow! Meow!'

Both children mewed and purred and sharpened their claws on the table leg. They even had to be given saucers of milk.

'Having a real kitten will be far more peaceful,' remarked their mother.

The Captain's Cabin

There were five sets of footprints in the wet sand, as the Garland family took their first walk along the beach. They had arrived at their boarding house only an hour ago, had their supper, unpacked, and now the children demanded a walk before bedtime.

Mr Garland's footprints were large and firm. Mrs Garland's were narrow and light. The two girls' prints were nearly the same size as there was only a year between them, and Joey, the youngest, left small prints in a straight line because he always ran everywhere.

The children were ahead of their parents, when Linda looked back, over her shoulder.

'They're waving. They think we've gone far enough.'

'But Linda,' protested Lucy, 'it can't be half-an-hour yet, and they *said* half-an-hour. It's more like ten minutes.'

'Let's just go to that funny little cottage at the foot of the cliffs,' said Joey, 'just there and back.'

'We can't,' said Linda. 'Look, they're both waving, and calling. We can go there tomorrow.'

'There are thirteen tomorrows,' said Lucy contentedly. 'That sounds a nice lot.' She turned back with her sister.

Joey, finding himself out-numbered, made a wide, sweeping curve and ended up facing in a backward direction. They soon caught up with their parents.

'Oh, Mummy,' said Joey, 'we'd just discovered the loveliest little cottage, right on the beach.'

'A fisherman's cottage,' said Lucy.

'A smuggler's hide-out,' said Linda.

'It might have been a ruin. We weren't near enough to see properly. May we go there tomorrow?'

'I don't see why not, Joey,' said his mother.

The next day they all bathed and had a picnic on the beach. Afterwards, Mr Garland went to sleep reading the paper, and Mrs Garland lay blissfully back, listening to the waves and the seagulls.

The children were still full of energy and set to work building a dam across a natural lagoon. They found some old corks among the seaweed on the tide-line, and soon a fleet of boats was sailing in the harbour.

'Mine has a man on board,' said Joey, poking a match stick into his cork.

'Mine has a mast,' said Linda, 'and a flag,' she added, fixing a ribbon of seaweed to the end of a stick.

'Mine has cargo,' said Lucy, placing some shells on her deck. *'Quinquirime of Nineveh from distant Ophir,'* she chanted, having little idea what the words meant, but repeating them with pleasure.

Then there was a rustling and Mr Garland emerged from behind his newspaper.

'Who's for a walk? We can visit your smuggler's cottage.'

'Oh, Daddy, we've just been making our dam and now we are building a fleet.'

'We need a pier where the boats can tie up.'

'It won't take long.'

'Get on with your pier when we get back,' said their father. 'The beach is so empty that no one will interfere with your work. Are you coming?' he asked his wife.

'Of course. Let's all go. You children can run on if you like. We'll meet you at the smuggler's den. Don't go further till Daddy and I have caught you up.'

They left their shoes and picnic things on the groundsheet and set off, the children running ahead.

As they approached their objective, the children slackened their pace. The nearer they got, the more dismal and dilapidated the building became. But the roof was still on, with some of the slates missing, and there was still a little glass, dirty and broken, in some of the windows. Others had been boarded up.

'It must have been a dear little house once,' said Linda. 'How I should love to have lived there. It doesn't need a garden with all that lovely pink thrift growing around.'

'What does that notice say?' asked Joey, who could not read properly yet.

Lucy went nearer. DO NOT CLIMB ON THESE CLIFFS AS LANDSLIDES ARE FREQUENT. BY ORDER.

'I don't suppose we can get inside,' said Linda wistfully. 'No one has lived here for ages and ages.'

'We can try,' said Joey, hopefully.

'I want to light a fire of driftwood and see the smoke pour out of the chimney.'

'What a surprise for the seagulls sitting on the roof,' said Lucy.

The seagulls flew off with a flap and a scream, as the children clustered round the door.

'It's padlocked.'

'It *was*, you mean. The padlock is just hanging.'

'Someone gave it a great whang with a stone, I should think.'

'Anyhow, the door will open—' Linda pulled it '– a little way, at least. We can squeeze in. It looks rather dark inside.'

She squeezed in, followed by Lucy, and Joey, hand in hand.

The inside was disappointing. The floor was uneven with loose stones lying about. The place smelt like a cave, stuffy and damp, fishy and vaguely unpleasant.

'I don't like it – much,' said Joey. 'I'd rather be outside looking in, than inside looking out.'

'Well, you can't see out properly. The windows are mostly boarded up. Somebody wanted to keep us out—'

'Or the sea out—'

'Or themselves safe in.'

The fireplace was filled with rubbish and Linda no longer wanted to make a fire. Or not that day, at any rate. Perhaps, when the strangeness had worn off, or when her parents were there too. But not now.

The children lingered a few minutes, neither enjoying themselves nor ready to leave. Their dreams of smugglers and fishermen and cosy times inside died hard. Suddenly there was a sharp, rapping on one of the windows looking seawards. Then an equally sharp rapping on the window next to the cliff. Then an even sharper, more hollow, series of raps on the back window which was boarded up.

All three children started in surprise and terror. Lucy and Joey, already holding hands in their uneasiness, hurled themselves into Linda's arms.

'It must be Daddy teasing us,' said Linda firmly. 'Who else could it possibly be? Daddy, where are you? You gave us a horrible fright. Come inside and see what it's like.'

The only reply was some rapid knocks on the door. The little group moved to the partly open door and looked out. There was no one there. To make matters worse, they could see their parents in the distance, bending down to look at something.

'It's horrid,' sobbed Joey. 'I said it was horrid at the very beginning, but no one took any notice.'

Linda ruffled his curls absently, then bent down and kissed him. Lucy, her blue eyes dark with fear, still clutched his other hand.

Linda still stood by the door. 'Don't move, anyone. Don't move. I want to think.'

'Why must you think? Let's run quickly to Mother. Don't let's hang about this hateful place,' pleaded Lucy. 'Why must we stay here while you think? Let's get away. What have you seen, Linda? Tell us. What is it?'

'Look,' said Linda. 'What can you see?'

'Just sand and the rocks behind. What else is there to see?'

'Don't you see, sillies! There are no footmarks except ours leading up the beach to the door. Look under the windows. Not a mark.'

'He must have been on the roof,' said Joey, through his tears. 'And he may be there still.'

'He – it – must have got on to the roof somehow. There's sand all round, under every window, and he would have to have trodden on it. I don't like it.'

The children were silent, each with their own thoughts. Joey was so used to marvellous events, being only five, that his only fear was that someone nasty – someone unfriendly – was near by and had tried to frighten him. That was horror enough. But the girls were trying to cope with something beyond their experience. Someone who left no prints on the soft sand. Who could rap on windows on different sides of the house simultaneously. Someone different from themselves, who did not wish them well.

'All right,' said Linda. 'Let's go back to Mummy and Daddy.'

Still holding hands, with Joey in the middle, they started running. Not one of them looked back, as their feet made deep marks in the soft sand.

When they reached their parents, it seemed odd to find them calm and unruffled as always. Joey had stopped crying, but the tears lay on his rosy cheeks.

'What is it, old chap? Have you hurt yourself?' Mr Garland took him up in his arms.

'No,' whispered Joey.

'We went into the little cottage and he didn't like it,' explained Linda. 'It was dark and smelly.'

'And someone rapped on the window,' put in Lucy. 'On several windows.'

'And we thought it was you, Daddy, and we called out—'

'But it wasn't anyone. There were no footprints. I'll never go there again. Never. Not ever.'

'Calm down,' said Mrs Garland. 'I expect you were trespassing and someone was trying to scare you off. After all, it's private property. Was there a notice up saying PRIVATE?'

'No,' said Linda. 'Only a big notice saying don't climb on the cliffs as they might fall down.'

'Well, it was private in a way,' said Lucy. 'There was a padlock on the door—'

'But it was broken. Someone had broken it. So we just walked in. Anyone could have walked in.'

'The door stuck half-way and we sort of squeezed in,' added Joey.

'It's obvious you weren't supposed to be there,' said their father, 'but you didn't break in and you weren't doing any harm. There was no need to frighten you. Most uncalled for. I think it was probably some village boys playing a trick. That's what it was. Don't you think I'm right?'

'They were on the roof,' said Joey with conviction.

With one accord, they retraced their steps along the beach as no one wanted to see the smuggler's den again at close quarters. The tide was coming in and the lagoon was deepening and widening.

'We'll have to have another harbour on the shore side,' decided Linda. 'Help us, Daddy.'

They all dug and hollowed out while Joey and Mrs Garland searched for more corks. The fleet grew to twenty vessels, riding at anchor in the new harbour, but just before teatime the sea won the battle. It rushed in, swirling and foaming first round their ankles, then round their knees. They had to retreat.

'Let's do it again tomorrow,' suggested Lucy. 'Let's start early, directly after breakfast, and we'll have all day for the harbour and the docks.'

'And I'll fortify it all,' said Joey, who had just learned a new word. 'I'll be the fortifying boy, I will.'

Joey fell asleep directly he was tucked up, but the girls talked for some time.

'I suppose it was like Daddy said – rough boys trying to scare us off.'

'Don't be an idiot, Lucy,' said Linda. 'You know it wasn't boys. How did boys move round with no feet? I just kept quiet because Joey was so frightened, and because I didn't want to worry Mummy. I still don't want to.'

'Oh, Linda, do let it be boys. I'm not afraid of rough boys. I don't like them much, but I'm not afraid of them. Linda, will you open the door a bit wider? Then the landing light will shine in.'

'Open it yourself. Your bed is nearer.'

'I daren't.'

'Then I'll do it.' Linda leapt out of bed and another few

inches of light fell on to the carpet. There was silence for a long time, but neither child was asleep.

'Oh, all right!' whispered Linda. 'It was boys – boys – boys. Only boys. Now go to sleep.'

'Thank you, Linda,' said Lucy, and fell asleep in a few seconds.

Then there was only Linda left lying awake, staring at the shaft of light, and thinking.

The next few days were hot and sunny and no one wanted to do anything except be on the beach, sunbathing, playing in the lagoon, and swimming three times a day. Lucy swam her first six strokes, and Joey learned to float, his fair curls fanning out in the water like fine seaweed.

Collections of various kinds were started; shells and seaweed and what they called 'treasure trove', which consisted of anything interesting washed up by the tide.

'Is it flotsam or jetsam?' asked Joey seriously, holding up a green, glass bottle.'

'Flotsam because it floats,' said Lucy.

'Jetsam because someone threw it in,' said Linda.

'I shall call it treasure trove,' said Joey, adding it to his pile of oddments.

Then, one afternoon, the sea-fret blew up and even Joey submitted to wearing an extra jersey.

'Let's have a brisk walk,' said Mr Garland. 'It's not really wet – just damp – and too chilly to hang about.'

'Let's go to the cabin,' said Lucy, whose courage had come back, boosted by the presence of two grown-ups.

'Yes, let's,' said Linda, who wanted to test several private ideas she had had.

'I won't go in,' announced Joey, suddenly overcome by a nameless dread. 'Or only holding Mummy's hand.'

THE CAPTAIN'S CABIN

They walked quickly, but the children, as usual, got ahead. When the cottage came into sight, Joey ran back to his father and mother, and held a hand of each. But the girls ran on and got there first.

'Let's go in again, Lucy. Daddy and Mummy are pretty near. Let's walk round first, or I will, and then we'll go in together.'

'Let's *both* walk round.'

'No,' said Linda firmly. 'One must stay by the door. Who shall it be?'

'Oh, I'll stay by the door. You go round, Lindy, but be quick. You'd better sing as you go.'

Linda darted round the building, singing 'Over the sea to Skye'.

'Not a sign of anyone or anything. Now we'll go in. It won't feel strange this time because it's our second visit.'

They went inside, to be greeted by the same damp, stuffy atmosphere, and the same unpleasant, fishy smell.

'It seems kind of harmless today,' whispered Lucy.

'It seems more ordinary,' agreed Linda. 'But look out of this window. Whatever is wrong out there? What can have happened to the others?'

Their father and mother were running towards the cottage, heads down, and their father snatched up Joey in his arms and Joey appeared to be burying his face in his father's shoulder.

'How could you be so stupid and careless,' said their mother crossly, as she joined them, panting and upset. 'I suppose you thought it was funny.'

'It's one of the first things sensible children learn,' said their father, following her, equally put out. 'Never, never to throw stones at people, only at things.'

'But Daddy, we never threw a thing—'

'Why ever should we?'

'Whatever happened?'

'You might have blinded Joey,' said their mother severely.

'Oh, Mother, do listen.' Linda spoke emphatically. 'We never threw anything at anybody, not even a pebble as big as a pea. And you actually believed we might have thrown a stone *at* Joey? You must be mad – both of you.'

Their father and mother looked taken aback.

'It didn't seem likely,' said their mother apologetically.

'But it looked as if it was happening,' said their father. 'A shower of small stones fell all round us – some of them hit us – and they came from your direction. What would you expect us to think?'

'Not what you did,' said Linda, angrily. 'It was inexcusable.'

'Well you know it wasn't us,' added Lucy. 'So that's all right.'

But they all knew it wasn't all right. The stones were real. They had been thrown by someone who wanted to hurt.

'Of course Lindy and Lucy didn't throw stones at me,' said Joey, in a matter of fact voice. 'It was that other man, the one in blue, with a handkerchief on his head, walking up and down outside the cottage. He did it. I saw him. It was that old man.'

All the questioning in the world couldn't get any more information out of Joey, except the sudden conviction that the man wore ear-rings, 'like a lady'.

'Are you sure you saw him, Joey,' said his father. 'You were hiding your face in my jersey most of the time.'

'I'm sure. He did this.' Joey strutted up and down with his hands clasped behind his back, stamping his feet and shaking his head, as if displeased. 'Then he did this.' Joey stooped down and threw stones as fast as he could pick them up.

'There are no footprints,' said Mrs Garland, looking at the sand in front of the cottage. 'Just the single line of Linda's when she ran round before going in. And everyone's in the doorway.'

'There weren't any footprints before,' said Linda, 'when we were here on our own and he rapped on the windows.'

'And you said it was village boys,' said Lucy, accusingly.

Just then there were some sharp knocks on the back window. Mr Garland was out of the door in a flash.

'Nothing there,' he said, coming slowly back. 'Nothing and no one.'

'Let's go back inland,' said Mrs Garland. 'I've had enough

of the beach. We all have. We'll have some chocolate and turn back.'

Nearer to the village, there were steep steps up to the cliff side, leading to a wooded valley where there were some good climbing trees. The sea-fret was dispersing and a gleam of sun appeared.

When they got back to the boarding house, the proprietor, Mr Mackay, was mowing the lawn. He was always ready for a chat, and stopped the machine with a smile.

'Can you tell us anything about that ruined cottage on the beach?' asked Mr Garland.

'Oh, you mean the Captain's Cabin? That's what it's always been called locally. There are so many rumours that I find it hard to tell fact from fiction. But it seems pretty certain that an old sea captain lived there – or some kind of sea-faring man. He lived there during his shore leaves, and settled there for good when he retired. He hated people poking and prying round the place. I've heard that he rapped on the windows and cursed to scare mischievous children away, and he threw stones at grown-ups. He was a crusty old devil, everyone's agreed on that.'

'Did he throw stones at you?' asked Linda.

'Oh, he was dead and buried before I was born. But the cabin still has a bad name. When I was a lad, we used to dare each other to go and knock on the door. Of course we frightened each other, though a friend of mine said he saw the captain walking up and down outside at dusk, muttering and shaking his head. Once, when I was peering in a window, I swear I felt a heavy hand on my shoulder. Just a lively imagination, of course,' he added hastily, seeing the round eyes of the listening children.

'Had he a wife, or did he live there alone?' asked Mrs Garland.

'He had no woman there, but the story goes that his old First Mate lived there for a time. People said the pair of them had found some treasure and they had hidden it in, or near, the cabin. That's why they never left the place together.'

'What happened to the First Mate, please?' asked Joey.

'Now that's a mystery, if you like. He simply disappeared. No one saw him leave. There was no funeral. He's never been heard of from that day to this. Never will be, if my guess is right.'

'Tell us your guess, please do,' begged Lucy.

'No, your guess is as good as mine, so guess away.'

Mr Mackay started up the motor again, but as he moved off, he called over his shoulder:

'I'll tell you one thing that isn't guess or imagination. My dog Dodger won't go near the cabin. He whines and his hair bristles when we go by. I've thrown stones for him to chase, but if they go within a few yards of it, he won't fetch them. He won't even fetch his ball, which is his dearest possession.'

Dodger lay asleep on the front steps, looking as fat and comfortable as any dog could, fed on a diet of nourishing scraps. It was difficult to picture him whining and cringing with fear.

The children longed to hear more, and began lying in wait for Mr Mackay, to ply him with more questions, till their parents forbade them to worry him.

'He's told you all he knows,' said Mr Garland, 'and he's a very busy man. Be content.'

During the last three days of their stay, there were high winds, high tides, and continual heavy rain. It was impossible even to go to the one shop for stamps or postcards without dressing up in wellingtons and sou'westers. The children played cards and Joey, unwilling to be left out of *Happy*

Families, miraculously learned to read overnight. The only thing he could not manage was holding his cards in a fan in his hand. He retired behind the sofa to spread them out on the floor.

'We'll always remember these holidays because Joey learned to read,' said Mrs Garland.

'And for the Captain's Cabin,' said Lucy, who still found getting to sleep a problem.

The last night was so stormy that everyone found sleep almost impossible. The wind howled, the waves crashed, and slates flew off the roof. Joey went into his parents' bed, and the two girls talked off and on all night. When the Garlands came down to breakfast, Mr Mackay was full of news of the damage.

'There's a cliff fall at last,' he said, 'and all the notices warning of "danger" are buried under earth and rock. That stretch of beach will never be the same again.'

'And the Captain's Cabin?' asked Linda.

'That's buried too. Gone as if it had never existed. I thought it would hold out till the winter storms, but this August one was too much. Force 11 gale.'

'Remember that,' said their father. 'You've experienced a Force 11 gale.'

At Christmas time, the Garland family received a Christmas card from the Mackays and Mr Mackay had written inside:

> 'When they were clearing away some of the cliff-fall behind the Captain's Cabin, they found a box with a skeleton in it, but no gold.'

'It was the First Mate,' said Linda. 'The horrid old captain murdered him. Then he could keep all the treasure for himself.'

'Let's go back next year and look for the treasure,' said Joey. 'May we, Daddy?'

'We'll see,' said Mr Garland. 'Mr Mackay would be glad if we did.'

'Mrs Mackay said you were well-behaved children,' added their mother.

'Then we'd better go before she changes her mind,' said Lucy. 'It's nice to be appreciated.'

'And we can find out if dear old Dodger still shivers and shakes when he goes by that bit of beach,' said Linda.

'*I* think the ghost is buried under the cliff-fall,' said Lucy, contentedly. 'Buried full fathom five.'

The Sunset Call

The Temple family had been staying on the shores of Loch Sheen for two weeks, before their father could leave his work and join them. It was the children's Easter holidays, but though early in the year, the little country hotel was full. By the time their father arrived, they were well dug-in. Mrs Temple had evolved a peaceful life for herself, walking and climbing with the three children, and also enjoying periods of reading and writing by herself.

As for the children, the days were not half long enough. When their father arrived, there was so much to tell him and show him, that he was almost deafened.

At last they paused for breath. 'It all sounds idyllic,' he remarked, as he drained the coffee pot. He had come over on the night ferry and was having breakfast. 'Jane likes being called "Mistress Temple". Henry wants to climb a mountain 2,219 ft high. Jilly can do Fair Isle knitting. And Ferdie has found some interesting minerals and is now going to be a geologist instead of a – what was the previous idea? – a jockey.'

'I may be a fisherman,' said Ferdie doubtfully. 'Angus says he'll take me out in his lobster boat.'

That evening, when Mr and Mrs Temple were going to bed, Mr Temple asked suddenly:

'Who, for heaven's sake, is Miss MacDuff? She looks ordinary enough, with that smooth dark hair and pale, serious

THE SUNSET CALL

face, but it's obvious she's cast a spell on the children. Is she a witch?'

'She may well be,' said Mrs Temple. 'From the first moment they set eyes on her, they've never left her alone for a minute. The other children in the hotel are just the same.'

'I could hardly believe my eyes this evening,' went on Mr Temple. 'When Henry suggested they had a game of chess, she gave one look at his hands and he added hastily: "After I've washed my hands, of course." And I saw Jilly show her that awful purple and yellow thing she is knitting, and she remarked: "Perhaps you should start again," and Jilly undid it without a moan. As for Ferdie, he showed me his box of minerals, beautifully arranged and named, and said: "Duffy looked up their names and wrote them out in script so I could copy them."

'I know,' said Mrs Temple in a puzzled voice. 'She just has a certain power. She ought to be head of a comprehensive school or something.'

'Perhaps she is.'

'Oh no. I once remarked that she knew a great deal and she replied, quickly: 'Oh, no. I left school at fifteen. I've been in private service.'

'Private service. I expect she's secretary to someone in the cabinet.'

'I doubt it. She's so unworldly.'

It was true. Sad, silent Miss MacDuff held a fascination for children of all ages. She had a way with the youngest guest, a toddler of eighteen months, and equally with a tall, silent youth who was waiting to go to university and was said to be a brilliant mathematician.

The next day, when the mountain had been climbed, the whole family, and Miss MacDuff, took a picnic tea by the loch in a sudden burst of hot sunshine. The children met together afterwards in the hotel.

'You see,' said Henry. 'It's just the same if we're out of doors as indoors.'

'Yes,' agreed Jilly. 'I noticed too. Just before six she said: "I think I'll start back to the hotel. I don't walk as fast as some of you."'

'And when mother said: "May I come with you?" she murmured something about liking to be alone for a while.'

'When we were in the hotel – remember the wet day? – she said she'd got some letters to write, and went upstairs.'

'I think there's some romantic reason,' said Jilly. 'Duffy had a lover – and he died – but they promised, before he died, to think about each other if they were apart.'

'I don't think she's romantic,' objected Henry.

'Of course you wouldn't! You think romance is film stars and platinum blondes and ice-skating champions. But it isn't.'

'Grown-ups have things they think are important and we don't,' said Ferdie suddenly. 'Like tidying their drawers and doing their nails, and things like that.'

'I'll find out before we leave,' said Henry. 'So there!'

'You can't *spy* on her, it's unfair. If her lover is dead, she may go away to mourn.'

Whatever the reason, Miss MacDuff liked to be alone for a little while about sunset, and excused herself most gracefully to attain her objective.

One pouring wet day (and there were several), when even the Temple family stayed indoors, Henry decided to put his intentions to the test. Though an honest, straightforward person at heart, he made up his mind to look through the keyhole of Miss MacDuff's door. He was not very hopeful, but all the bedrooms had keyholes, though no keys. The doors could be fastened by a small brass bolt, if necessary.

'I won't start on another game of Happy Families,' said Miss MacDuff gently to the circle of six children with whom she had been playing. 'There's something I ought to do before supper. Jilly, you help the ones who can't read very well.'

She walked, upright as ever, out of the room. When she had gone, Henry laid down his book and followed. He felt like a private eye, but a private eye with a conscience. Jilly's words had gone deep. But the desire to know was even deeper.

Henry and Jilly were not alone till after supper. The rain had stopped, but the loch was Prussian blue, with tiny white frills where the waves broke.

'Well, Henry. What did you see?'

'I didn't *see* anything. It's what I heard.'

'Tell me. Tell me quickly. Everyone's coming out for a breath now the rain's stopped.'

'I put my ear to the keyhole, as I could see nothing, and I heard bagpipes.'

'Why not? She was listening to her transistor.'

'She hasn't one. I found that out at supper.'

'Were they ghostly bagpipes?'

'How on earth should I know? As far as I'm concerned, bagpipes only play three tunes. A march – a dance – and a sad one.'

'Which was it?'

'I was too surprised to think. I'd say the sad one.'

'What do we do next?'

'You must do something next time. It's your turn. And you're more musical than me.'

'Oh nonsense. I play the piano, not the bagpipes.'

There were only three days left before the children went back to school. Jilly, for all her scruples, spent hours scheming and planning. She, too, must hear the ghostly bagpipes. But how? Then chance played into her hands.

They all went to the one town on the island to buy last postcards and paperbacks, and a colouring book for Ferdie. They invited Miss MacDuff, who accepted. The expedition included tea at a café and afterwards they had a last look at the harbour where the fishing fleet was riding at anchor. Then

THE PHANTOM ROUNDABOUT

they were to meet at the car at a quarter past six. The party split up, with promises not to be late. Jilly never took her eyes of Miss MacDuff who loitered, in a very natural way, on the quay, and then slipped off to a tiny public garden, with a few shabby seats and bare trees. She sat down on a bench and covered her eyes with her hands. Jilly, in crêpe-soled sandals, tiptoed behind some bushes. No bird sang and the branches hardly rustled. It was one of the few calm days they had had during their stay. Then, unmistakably, the haunting sound of bagpipe music filled the air. Miss MacDuff sat still as a statue. When the music ceased, she left her bench and walked quickly towards the place where the car was parked. Jilly followed at a distance.

Henry and she discussed what she had heard long after

THE SUNSET CALL

they were supposed to be asleep. Their rooms were next door and Henry slipped in to join her.

'Why? Why? Why?' they asked each other. 'And how?'

But they could find no answer.

'Scottish people are psychic,' persisted Jilly. 'Duffy may be the seventh child of a seventh child and have second sight.'

'This isn't second sight, it's second hearing,' corrected Henry.

'You know what I mean. Don't be tiresome. An ancestor may have fallen at – well at Culloden – and he died at sunset and ever since the seventh child has heard the bagpipes playing a lament at sunset. I bet that's it. I think it's a brilliant piece of deduction. Worthy of Sherlock Holmes.'

'A bit too brilliant!' said Henry. 'Too neat and tidy. You read too much romantic fiction.'

'Better than your horrible science fiction, only fit for a moron.'

On this perfectly friendly note, they separated. The grown-ups were beginning to come up to bed.

The last day was upon them before they were aware of it. When Ferdie heard they were leaving tomorrow, he wept unashamedly. Miss MacDuff made him an admiral's hat out of an old newspaper. 'Wear it this way, and you're Napoleon,' she declared. 'Or the other way, and you're Nelson.'

'Which shall I be?' wailed Ferdie, in an agony of indecision.

'I prefer Nelson,' said Miss MacDuff.

'Then I shall be that one,' said Ferdie happily.

At six o'clock, Miss MacDuff slipped out of the room, murmuring something about last-minute packing.'

'Now's the time,' said Henry to Jilly. 'Our very, very last chance. Now or never.'

'Oh, all right. But who will ask?'

'You'd better. Girls are always exchanging addresses. Seems more natural.'

They ran upstairs and Henry knocked gently on Miss MacDuff's bedroom door.

After a pause, she opened the door, pale and calm as usual.

'Duffy—' they both began together. 'May I have your address?' said Jilly. 'We'd all like it.'

'I gave it to your mother yesterday,' said Miss MacDuff, sounding slightly surprised. 'But of course you can have it too.'

She wrote a few lines on a page of her diary and tore it out.

'Wasn't there something else you wanted to know? I think there is. In fact I'm sure. You were far too clever for me, both of you.'

'It's about the bagpipe music at sunset,' blurted out Henry.

'But it doesn't matter,' said Jilly, in a panic. 'It's of no consequence. Please don't tell us. We were abominably curious. I feel dreadful.' She blushed scarlet.

'S-s-so do I.' Henry only stammered when in a state of acute embarrassment.

'Sit down, both of you. It's the most natural thing in the world that you should want to know. And I do believe it's the most natural thing in the world that I should tell you. One shouldn't keep things from one's friends, especially important things. But please don't tell Ferdie. It might upset him.'

'We haven't, and we won't ever.'

'I'm a children's nurse. I was for many years with the same family who lived in a castle on the edge of the sea. There were rocks down below and the sound of the waves filled every room. The family and their ancestors had lived there for a very long time. They had six little girls, and I was nurse to them all. Then a son was born. I won't describe all the rejoicings. Bonfires were lit and flags flown and the laird gave a party to all his people. They came from far and wide, in little boats from the neighbouring islands, to drink the health of their next laird.

'He was a bonny boy, what we call a bra' bairn, strong and vigorous. Not very big, but he sat up and rolled over and crawled much earlier than his sisters. And we called him Jock-in-the-box because he was so springy. One day, when he was eight months old, I was standing by a staircase window at sunset, with Jock in my arms. It was a hot day and the window was wide open. He was watching the seagulls fly past. All of a sudden, never ask me how, he gave a great leap of joy – out of my arms – down, down to the rocks below.

'The family never blamed me. No one blamed me. I just blamed myself as I shall do till my dying day. All the laird's people gathered again for his burial and after that, every day at sunset, the laird's piper walked up and down on the strip of rocky shore, playing a lament.

'I left the castle for ever, though the little girls begged me to stay, and the family begged me, too. But I knew I must go. I went secretly, at night. A friendly fisherman took me across to the mainland. I thought distance would do some good, putting time and the sea between. Yet every evening at sunset I hear the piper who is piping Jock's lament on that lonely shore. At first I thought it was in my head. Then I learned otherwise.'

Draw the Curtains

After Christmas, with all its excitements and treats, Luke and Clive always spent the New Year with their grandparents, who lived in the country. They had done this all their lives, and looked forward to their visits. At first their mother stayed with them, to keep an eye on them, but now they were older they stayed there by themselves.

'Are you sure you want to come?' their grandmother asked, on the telephone. 'You have so much at home that we can't provide, your friends and shops and cinemas and skating rinks and much else. Here there's nothing. Just two quiet old people living in a quiet, rather dull countryside. I shan't be offended if you don't come.'

'Oh *no*, Granny,' they said emphatically. 'We simply love coming to Holly Hall, and seeing you and Grandpa, and the lovely old house full of lovely old things. And the garden is such fun. We look forward to coming for ages before it happens. Has Grandpa bought anything since last time?'

'Yes, he has. At least he hasn't bought it but he's taken possession of it. No, I shan't tell you another word. You can see for yourselves.'

Their grandfather collected antiques and the boys took a keen interest in his purchases. One year there had been a carriage clock in a leather case, which struck the nearest hour if you pressed a plunger. Another time it was a writing desk with a secret top drawer. Once it was a Persian rug and

Grandpa told them that every genuine Persian rug had a dragon woven in it somewhere. They had searched for this dragon, but had never found it.

Besides the antiques, Luke and Clive loved the flat countryside with its empty roads where, in heavy frost, the ditches were iced over and were excellent for sliding.

This time, the moment they arrived, they began questioning their grandfather. 'What is it? Where is it? Can we see it?'

The reply was: 'Go off and look for yourselves. It's big enough.'

The boys went from room to room, first downstairs and then upstairs.

'It's not in our room,' said Luke. 'I remember everything in there perfectly.'

'Then we've missed it. And Grandpa said it was really big.'

'I know. We haven't been in the other bedroom at the end of the long corridor.'

They scampered off and opened the door of a room they very seldom entered. And there it was, beyond any doubt.

'Isn't it super, Luke.'

'I wonder if it's comfortable?'

'I wonder who used to use it.'

'Oh, dozens of people, I suppose. It looks so old.'

'Do you think they'll let us sleep in it?'

'I don't see why not. We'll persuade Granny. I bet no other boy we know has ever slept in a four-poster.'

They started on their persuasion at once.

'Granny, would you like to give us a marvellous treat – the most marvellous treat we've ever had?' began Luke.

'It won't cost you or Grandpa a penny, I promise you.'

'Or make any extra work.'

'You don't want to make a raft and sail it on the pond?' said Granny suspiciously. 'I can't allow that.'

'Oh no. It's safe as safe. We only want to sleep in the four-poster bed.'

'Aren't you comfortable in your usual beds?'

'Of course we are. But we'd like to be more than just comfortable. We'd like to be thrilled. Excited. We'd be doing something hardly anyone has ever done, who's alive now.'

'Do, please let us.'

'It's such an odd notion,' said Granny, sounding rather flustered.

'We won't bounce or play on it,' said Clive. 'We'll just lie still in it, like two logs.'

'I suppose you could,' said Granny, doubtfully. 'Your grandfather found it in the loft over the old stable, and had it repaired and renovated. I had curtains made as like the original ones as possible. I'll go and put a couple of hot water bottles in it, now. You can't be too careful.'

Their grandpa seemed rather taken by the idea and chuckled; so that evening they undressed in the blue room, as it was called, and settled down in the four-poster.

'Shall we draw the curtains, Luke?'

'Yes. Let's do it properly. You draw your side and I'll do mine.'

They felt very private and secret with the curtains drawn. Granny kissed them good night and they lay very still. But sleep seemed far away. They began to toss and turn and counted up to fantastic numbers, but they didn't even feel drowsy.

'What's wrong?' said Clive at last. 'This is hopeless. It will be morning before long.'

'No it won't. I heard the clock in the hall strike either eleven or twelve. I rather lost count.'

THE PHANTOM ROUNDABOUT

'Do you think someone died in this bed?' whispered Clive.

'As it's so old, lots of people must,' said Luke in a matter-of-fact voice. 'Especially when there weren't many hospitals.'

'Then it may be haunted and the ghost won't let us get to sleep. It can't rest so it won't let us rest, either.'

'I don't believe that. Ghosts are very uncommon and they usually come back because they're unhappy. They float about and moan and wail. But we haven't seen or heard a thing. Now have another try at getting to sleep and try to keep to your side of the bed. That'll be a help.'

This time Clive fell asleep, so Luke lay awake alone. He began to plan to make some furniture for his little sister's dolls' house. A table would be easy, he thought, and a bench and a bed. I'm glad I brought my tool set with me. There's bound to be some wood somewhere. I do wish Clive would stop sniffling and snuffling. He never does it when he's awake. I shall give him a poke in a minute. Then, as he listened, a horrible discovery dawned on him. As well as the sniffling and snuffling, he could hear deep, regular breathing. He was quite sure of this. There was somebody, or something alive, in the room with them, in the bed with them, the breathing sounded so very close.

Luke turned on his back so he could listen better, but there was no doubt. The more he strained his ears the clearer it sounded. He decided to wake Clive and let him hear it too.

'Clive! Clive! Wake up! I want to tell you something.'

Waking Clive was not easy as he was in his first, deep sleep, but proddings and shakings succeeded in the end.

'Is it morning?' asked Clive sleepily. 'It feels just like the middle of the night.'

'No, it isn't morning. Now wake up properly and listen. Can you hear something strange quite near to us.'

'No, Luke. Just your breathing and mine. What do you want me to hear?'

'Well, we must both hold our breath for as long as we can. Take a deep breath. Hold it. And remember to listen. Are you ready? Now.'

Both boys breathed in. They could have held their breath much longer but Clive could not bear to keep quiet.

'I could hear someone else breathing, very gently and evenly. Is that what you meant?'

'Yes, it was. I've been hearing it for quite a long time. Ever since you went to sleep.'

'Whatever is it, Luke? Do you think there's someone hiding in the room? I don't like this bed. I wish I was back in my own.'

'There can't be anyone hiding. There's only that old wooden cupboard and Granny opened it so we could hang our spare clothes in.'

'It might be a rat.' Clive's voice trembled a little.

'No,' said Luke. 'It keeps in the same place. Rats run about. But I'll turn the light on just the same. It must come from somewhere.'

They looked, carefully, all over the room, in every corner, and Clive insisted on turning back the bedclothes and examining the bed. The notion of a rat still lingered in his mind.

'Don't,' protested Luke. 'You'll let all the warmth out.'

'I must be quite sure there's nothing else to be let out – nothing alive. Otherwise I could never get to sleep again.'

When the search was over, they crept back to bed, turned off the light, and lay very still and very close together.

'It has stopped,' said Luke. 'Can you hear anything?'

'No, I can't. It's gone. Thank goodness.'

They were too relieved to talk any more and soon they were both fast asleep.

The next day, neither of them considered relating their experience to their grandparents. For one thing, in the daylight, it seemed improbable and they couldn't bear not to be believed. But daylight didn't shake their conviction that something ghostly and unusual had happened. Of that they were certain.

'It was a ghost breathing,' said Luke firmly. 'It must have been. There's no other explanation.'

'I don't like the idea of sharing my bed with a ghost,' said Clive. 'Shall we ask Granny if we can move back to our old beds?'

'Rather not!' said Luke indignantly. Daylight had made him feel very brave. 'It may be the ghost of someone who loved this bed so much that he sometimes comes back and visits it. Perhaps on his birthday. We may never hear him again. If we'd been asleep I'm sure his light breathing wouldn't have disturbed us. We should never have known he was there.'

As the day wore on, and the boys enjoyed climbing familiar trees and remaking a den they had made a year ago, Clive's courage came back too, and when they went to bed he didn't even suggest keeping the light on. They lay tense for a long while, straining their ears for the faintest sound. At last they relaxed and dropped off.

In the middle of the night, Luke woke. Immediately he heard the same soft, even breathing. He shook Clive and this time he woke more easily. They both listened. Then, in the darkness, they heard a thin, childish voice, speaking almost into their ears.

'It's a crying shame. I'm starving and I was just counting on a slice of game pie or a tart. Or even a pitcher of milk.'

Luke and Clive clutched each other's hands and had to

smother an exclamation of surprise when a second voice, equally high and childish and equally close, replied.

'So was I. I've been looking forward to a feast all day. I wonder who thought of locking the larder door. I don't think it was the cook. She seems a kindly woman.'

'I'll wager it was Uncle Silas. He always thinks of horrid things. That beastly, thin, lumpy gruel he ordered for our supper – that was his idea.'

'At least you weren't sick tonight. It's still inside you. You'd feel even hungrier if you'd thrown it up.'

'Do you think much about the time when our father and mother were alive – and we had our ponies – and our rabbits – and Master Foster came to teach us Latin?'

'Yes, of course I do. Nearly all the while. But I fear I've forgotten all my Latin. Those days are getting further and further away, like a dream. Didn't we wear different clothes then?'

'Yes. Very different from these patched rags. We had fur hats in the winter and long woollen hose.'

'I had a knife in a leather sheath. Where is it now? Oh Jervais, I can't bear living here with Uncle Silas and being always cold and hungry. And frightened.'

There was a sound of sobbing, half-smothered in the pillow.

'There, there, Francis. Don't give up. Things may get better. Remember what Father always said to us. "A man can bear what comes his way, with God's help".'

'But I'm not a man. I'm only a boy. And I never forget to say my prayers. I'm not brave.'

'Remember how brave you were when the ferret bit you. You never cried at all. Mother said you were braver than many men.'

'Oh Mother, Mother, come back!' sobbed Francis. 'I want you. I need you.'

'Lie close to me, Francis, and you'll get warm and we shall both get to sleep. Maybe we shall have pleasant dreams of the old life.'

'Then how shall we bear to wake, Jervais, and find we are still living in this one?'

The smothered sobbing went on for a little longer, getting fainter. At last there was silence, but once the ghost children were silent, the living boys began to talk.

'Isn't it awful,' said Clive, in a choking voice. 'They sounded as if they were children like us, or perhaps Jervais was a little older, I could kill that horrible Uncle Silas, the cruel wretch.'

'It isn't happening now,' said Luke. 'Or I don't see how it can be. It's all over and done with. It may have happened years and years ago. It's like history.'

'I shall never enjoy history lessons again,' said Clive. 'I shall always think the sad bits really happened to real people, like Jervais and Francis.'

'Well, so they did,' said Luke. 'It's our fault if we don't imagine them properly. Do you think we shall hear any more from the ghost boys? I should like to know what happened to them.'

'I think we shall. I think they'll go on talking – perhaps tomorrow. I'm sure I shall never get to sleep again tonight. I wonder what happened to their parents? I hope Mummy and Daddy are all right.'

'Of course they are. They rang us up yesterday evening.'

'So they did. Goodnight, Luke.'

In the end, what they had heard stopped going round and round in their heads and they fell asleep, and had to be woken by their granny the following morning.

The next two nights in the four-poster were uneventful. No breathing. No sobbing. No voices. But during the third night both boys woke simultaneously and listened, spell-bound, once more, to the ghostly dialogue.

'That's the end,' said Jervais in a firm tone. 'I won't let Uncle Silas strike you again. I've made up my mind.'

'It didn't hurt – much,' said Francis. 'My cheek is only sore when I press it. I shall sleep on the other side. I can bear it.'

'But I can't. Striking you across the face for taking a spoonful of honey. Your cheek is bruised and swollen already and it will be worse tomorrow. How dared he strike his elder brother's son, his own flesh and blood. And to call you a thief, to boot.'

'I thought he was going to turn on you when you called him a brute.'

'He daren't,' said Jervais defiantly. 'He saw from my face that he had gone too far. If only there was someone we could go to for advice. But Uncle has no friends and he won't admit any of ours. He's driven all our own family friends away. I've heard him giving orders that nobody is to be admitted. And that savage wolfhound is enough to keep people from approaching. We must have money of our own, or money that will be mine when I am of age. I don't understand it.'

'Jervais, do you ever think that he doesn't want us to grow up? That he hopes we may die before then? When the physician came to lance a maid's boil, he said: "Don't let the boys play near that pond. It is unwholesome. Noisome vapours rise from it and they may catch a low fever." But Uncle often says to us: "Go and play by the pond. You can do no mischief there." '

'He *wants* us to catch a fever.'

'We won't catch a fever just to please him. We won't stay here. We'll soon be miles and miles away from that pond and its noisome vapours. We're going to run away to sea. And we're going tomorrow. I've made up my mind.'

'Tomorrow, Jervais?'

'Yes, tomorrow. Uncle will be away for two days, putting in an appearance at court. I saw his servant airing his best clothes and the sewing woman working at his linen. We may have to wait a long time for such a good chance to occur again.'

'But Jervais. Where is the sea? We've never even set eyes on it. And how can we find a ship? People will think we are beggar boys in these tattered garments.'

'Let them. A captain will be far more likely to take us on as cabin boys if he thinks we are poor and no one will ask questions and try to get us back. I've worked it all out. Now listen. No, don't turn your head or you'll upset the wet cloth I've laid on your cheek. Just lie still and listen.'

'Very well, Jervais. I'm listening.'

'I've found out from a map in the library that Harwich is the nearest port. We'll take two horses and ride a good part of the way. Then we'll turn the horses loose in some wild place where they won't be traced too easily, and we'll go the rest of the journey on foot.'

'But what if someone sees us leave the Hall?'

'They won't. I know the servants are all planning to enjoy themselves while their master is away. They are all going to the fair in the next village. No one will miss us. When they get home they'll think we are asleep in bed, and they'll most of them be drunk, no doubt. If luck is on our side, we shall have the place to ourselves for a few hours. We can take a good stock of provisions and other useful things.'

'You make it sound like a story. Like a true story that really happened.'

'And it will really happen, soon. Think of being free. Ships biscuits and salt pork will be better than that foul gruel. And we shall be among honest men.'

'You won't ever leave me, Jervais?'

'Of course not. We shall stay together. I shall only sign on if the captain will take us both. I've heard that sailors are kind to children. Most of them are married with wives and children of their own, and that makes their hearts tender. We've only to do what we are told and work hard and keep a civil tongue in our heads, and all will be well. We may be officers one day, who knows?'

'Shall we sail to foreign lands and see coral islands and coconut palms and crocodiles?' Francis's voice sounded eager.

'All that and much more. Parrots and monkeys and flying fish. All the wonders that mother used to read to us about in that book called *The Wonders of the World*.'

'Why are you lighting the candle, Jervais?'

'I'm going to carve our names somewhere before we go, yours and mine. I've kept my sharp, little knife with the worn blade. I'll do it here, behind the bedpost, low down.'

Luke and Clive heard the sound of wood being cut away. It went on for a long time.

'There!' said Jervais triumphantly. JERVAIS AND FRANCIS 1780. We'd better choose a new surname for our new life. GRAEME might give us away.'

'Let's have an heroic one. What about Cranmer? He was a martyr and very brave.'

'All right. It's not too unusual to be questioned.'

'Jervais Cranmer. Francis Cranmer. How strange it sounds.'

'It'll sound natural enough when we hear other people using it.'

'Goodnight, Jervais. My face doesn't throb any more.'

'Goodnight, Francis. Let's say our prayers before we sleep.'

The two voices said the Lord's Prayer, Francis sounding half asleep.

DRAW THE CURTAINS

'God bless and keep my brother and me and help me to do the right thing,' added Jervais. Then silence reigned between the curtains of the four-poster.

Next morning, Luke and Clive had to search hard to find the two carved names and the date. They had become discoloured with time. But they were clearer when they had gone over them with a pin, picking out dust and dirt.

'Grandpa,' said Luke at breakfast. 'Can you please tell us some family history. We'd like so much to know.'

'And especially if there were any ancestors called Jervais and Francis,' added Clive.

'Why this interest all of a sudden,' said their grandfather, laying down his paper.

'Because of some carving we found on the four-poster bed. We'll show you after breakfast.'

'Well I never,' said their grandfather later, on his knees at the head on the bed, with a torch in his hand. 'Trust you to discover something that everyone else has missed. You've sharp eyes, the pair of you.'

'Can you please try to find out something about them,' begged Luke again. 'When you have time,' he went on politely.

'I've a whole drawer full of papers in the desk, beside all the legal papers that are kept at the bank. There are old letters and extracts from journals and all kinds of things. I've never been through them carefully. That date, 1780, should be a help. Otherwise I wouldn't know where to begin.'

'When will you go through them?' inquired Luke. 'Couldn't we both help you?'

'No, I'm afraid you couldn't. Many of the pages are torn and mended, with the ink faded, and difficult to read. I'll try to find time during the day. You've made me curious.'

'Will you start now?'

But their grandfather had other plans for that morning, and it was after supper when he settled himself in the library, with the contents of the drawer spread out on the desk. The boys said a reluctant goodnight and went slowly up to bed. They would have been relieved to know that their grandfather became totally absorbed in his task and stayed up till the early hours of the morning.

'What did you find?' asked Clive eagerly, the next day at breakfast.

'Not a great deal, but more than I had hoped.'

'Please tell us. We can't bear to wait.'

'Just give me a chance to put the papers in order. I read so late last night that I left them all over the place. I'll call you when I'm ready.'

The boys spent most of the waiting period talking and wondering about the ghost children. Did they get away safely? Had they met with a kind captain who had taken them on as cabin boys? Were they sea-sick? Had Uncle Silas attempted to find them? There were so many questions. So many possibilities. They made up stories to fit them all. As soon as their grandfather called they hurried to join him.

'I can't think why I've not sorted through these papers before. I find them absorbing,' began their grandfather. 'Well, to start with, Samuel Graeme was squire here during the latter half of the eighteenth century, and he and his wife, Phoebe, were drowned in a skating accident in 1778. They left two sons, Jervais and Francis. Jervais was the heir, but as he was only a child his Uncle Silas became his guardian till he came of age. Silas came to live at the Hall and look after the place.

'It's clear that this Silas was an unsavoury character. There seem to have been many scandalous stories about him – shooting a villager for stealing firewood – trouble with young maids employed at the Hall – a real bad lot. He was killed in a duel in 1800.'

'And the boys? What happened to them, Grandpa?'

'Now that's a real mystery. They seem to have disappeared completely. There's no grave bearing their name in the churchyard. Nothing. They may have died away from home, or even abroad. All I know is that Jervais never took up his inheritance. The place went to a cousin called Webster. And there have been Websters at Holly Hall ever since. I hope when it's your turn, Luke, you'll be rich enough to have the roof repaired. It would cost too much for me and I doubt whether your father will manage it either, when he takes my place.'

'Thank you, Grandpa. Thank you very very much. Is there anyone in the village who knows about past history? Anyone we could ask? I'd love to know a little more, if it were possible.'

'Yes, Luke, you could ask the vicar. No, not the present young man who is too busy raising money for the new bells to bother about the past. I mean the dear old vicar, Canon Peters, who was vicar here for over forty years. He's a great antiquarian and he loves to talk. He lives in the cottage next the sweet shop.'

'May we visit him this afternoon?'

'Why not? Give him time to have his nap after lunch – he's over eighty. Go about half-past three. He's fond of children and won't turn you away.'

The boys found that Canon Peters gave them a warm welcome and was interested in their grandfather's discoveries and in the names and date carved on the four-poster. He, too, had heard scandalous stories about Silas Graeme, who was a black-hearted villain.

The boys almost recounted their ghostly experiences, but they had decided on the way to keep them secret for the time being. They confined themselves to asking the Canon if he had ever come across the names Jervais and Francis Cranmer.

A puzzled look came over the old man's face.

'They remind me of something,' he said, 'but I can't for the moment recall exactly what. It'll come back to me presently. It always does. That's one of the penalties of being old.'

Just then the housekeeper brought in a delicious tea and conversation lapsed for the time being. Then, as the boys were eating a last buttered crumpet, the Canon suddenly exclaimed:

'I've got it! I've got it! I told you I'd remember in a few minutes. You know the drinking fountain on the green?'

'Yes,' said both boys together.

'The inscription on it is almost defaced, but when I first came to this village as a young man, I was very keen on such things, and I spent some hours examining it with a lens and in the end I made it out. The mason hadn't cut the letters deep enough. It reads:

> *Given by Captain Jervais Cranmer R.N.*
> *and his brother Francis Cranmer, merchant. 1820*

'I did my best to find out who these benefactors were, but I failed. It was thought that they had some connection with the village, but no one knew what. There was a Captain Cranmer who commanded the frigate *Resolute* and fought under Nelson. Anyhow, it was a kind and generous act and the fountain still works well over a hundred and fifty years later. Sure you won't have another slice of cake? Another cup of tea?'

The boys thanked Canon Peters and went back to Holly Hall past the fountain. The inscription was almost unreadable.

'We might try and clean the letters tomorrow,' said Luke.

'Yes, we will. Just think, we may be the only people alive who know why the Cranmer brothers gave the fountain. Didn't Jervais do well to rise from cabin boy to captain?'

'I suppose Francis didn't like the sea much. Anyhow, being a merchant means he still had dealings with ships,' said Luke.

'Weren't they brave? I think Jervais was simply great. And Francis was jolly good for a younger brother. He never wavered. Shall we ever tell father and mother what we overheard in the four-poster?'

'Let's wait and see. When we get home we may know what to do for the best. It was so real to us, but what would it sound like to someone else?'

'That's the question,' said Clive.

The White Pony

'Is this field ours, as well as the garden, Mummy?'

Jessie stood beside her mother at the bottom of the garden of their new house, and looked over the hedge as she asked the question. Beyond the hedge stretched a green uneven meadow. Beyond the meadow was the lane where the traffic went by.

'Yes. It's ours. But Daddy lends it to a farmer who grazes his horses there sometimes. Aren't they beauties?'

'Yes, they are. Just the colour of a shiny chestnut. I've never understood before why some horses are called chestnut. Shall I be able to have a pony of my own now we've got a field for him? Terry would like one too.' Terry was her brother.

'Perhaps. When you're a little older and have had a few riding lessons. And when you can look after him properly. Just look at those two racing around. They're full of high spirits.'

'Yes, they're lovely. But I like the little white one best.'

'White what, darling?'

'White pony, of course.'

A change came over Mrs Parker's face. She looked suspicious and uneasy. She began to say; 'Oh, but—' Then changed her mind and stopped.

'There are two worlds we live in,' she said presently. 'The real world, we all share, where those two horses belong, and

then there's the world of imagination where fairies and story books and your little white pony belong. You'll have to learn to keep them separate. We all have to learn. You know what I mean?'

'Yes, I do. You mean I tell lies and you don't like to say so. You're ashamed of having a child who tells lies.'

'No, darling. I don't mean that. To you, both worlds overlap sometimes.'

'They don't! I know exactly what is real and what isn't. So there!'

Her mother went back to the house and Jessie stayed by the hedge, staring at the horses. She was glad when Terry came along.

'Terry. Look at those horses in the field. How many can you see?'

'Two, of course. Two brown ones. There seems to be something white in the far corner. Perhaps a foal? Or a donkey? It's moving, so it must be alive.'

'It's a white pony, silly. I can see it perfectly. Its black hoofs and its flowing tail and everything. Why can't you?'

'The white one is fading away. But I did see something. I told you.'

Terry went off with his catapult. He only aimed at trees and posts and tin cans, never at anything alive, but Jessie found herself wondering what would happen if he aimed at the white pony. Would the stone go right through it? Would the pony mind? She nearly called Terry back to ask him to try the experiment. But there was always the chance that the white pony could feel, could bleed, even. She didn't know whom she could ask. It must be someone who would just answer and not start investigating and cross-examining her.

'Daddy,' she said at teatime, can ghosts feel?'

'I've never seen a ghost, so I've not had first-hand experience. I doubt it. They can walk through doors and walls, so they can't collide with material objects and feel pain like we do.'

'Can they – can they bleed?'

'Oh no. Some of them are said to carry their heads under their arms, if they were beheaded in life, but I've never heard of there being any blood about.'

'How can you talk with such confidence about something you don't believe in?' objected his wife. 'You'll muddle the children up.'

'I'm talking quite seriously about what I've heard and read. Not what I've seen.'

'We've done *Macbeth* at school,' said Terry, 'and in one place, in a scene with the witches, Macbeth sees the ghost of a bloody child. So they can bleed.'

'It doesn't say a "bleeding" child,' corrected his father.

'That's enough. No more ghosts and ghouls tonight. Anyone like some more cheese?'

Jessie saw her mother was uneasy. 'I bet she half believes in ghosts herself,' she thought, 'but she won't own up.'

Jessie had been familiar with ghosts for a long time, not just in stories, but from experience. When she let Snowball, her pet rabbit, on to the grass for a run, she often saw another rabbit, a blotchy one, playing with her. And when Micky, her white mouse, died, and left Minnie a lonely widow, she knew that Micky often visited her at night. She had seen him. But all this was so ordinary and natural that only other people's disbelief made it extraordinary, and rather shocking.

She had never, up till now, seen the ghost of a person, though she looked – in vain – for a cowled figure when visiting Fountains Abbey or other likely ruins. Once, she thought she heard ghostly music, but Terry had pointed out that it was someone's transistor.

In the days that followed, the white pony was often grazing with the chestnut horses. The chestnuts came racing to the gate in the hedge, hoping for sugar lumps or an apple, and in time the white pony came too, when the others had cantered off, munching contentedly.

'Have a sugar lump, Clover?' Jessie coaxed. She had decided, if she ever had a pony of her own, to call her Clover. Clover nuzzled her hand and lowered her head to have her forehead scratched, but the sugar lump stayed on Jessie's palm, damp and uneaten. Food was of no interest.

One morning, Jessie got up very early and let herself out into the quiet, sunny morning. The horses were feeding peacefully on the far side of the field, next the lane. Clover was near the garden hedge.

'Clover. Come to the gate. I've had an idea.'

Clover came slowly and cautiously, stepping sideways.

'Stand still. We're going for a ride, you and me. I only weigh three stone three pounds, so I shan't be too heavy. Steady, now. I'm not used to riding bareback.' (I'm not very used to riding at all, she added to herself. Only two lessons.) 'That's better. Let me get my leg over. I think I'm all right. Please, please don't buck me off. Help me.'

All the time she fondled Clover's neck, patting her and stroking her, and talking softly and reassuringly.

'Let's be off. Gently does it!' She pressed slightly with her knees. Clover gave a nicker of pleasure and set off, stepping carefully, as if she knew she had a learner on her back. She broke into a trot. Jessie continued to feel safe. Then she tried a brisk canter – that was more difficult. Jessie's two plaits bounced up and down on her shirt, and her three stone three pounds bounced up and down on Clover's wide, warm back. It was a glorious experience, full of shared satisfaction.

Not a gallop, she murmured to herself. That would be

tempting fate. Trotting and cantering – yes. Galloping – no. Clover read her thoughts and kept up her lively canter, miraculously avoiding the molehills and tussocks of grass. Or perhaps going through them?

When their ever-increasing circles took in the far side of the field, beside the lane, Clover went dangerously near the chestnuts. Jessie watched anxiously for their reaction, but none came. They never lifted their heads from the grass they were cropping, and never turned their gleaming necks.

They can't see me, a live girl on a ghost pony, marvelled Jessie. They can't see us or hear us. But Clover and I can see and feel each other. Clover stood still as a statue while Jessie slid off her back.

Jessie arrived for breakfast with rosy cheeks and shining eyes.

'Remind me to do your hair properly after breakfast,' said her mother. 'One plait is quite undone.'

'I've been—' Jessie was going to say riding, but changed it to 'playing – in the paddock with the horses. With *all* the horses,' she repeated defiantly. 'The white pony is sweet. So gentle and friendly. But she doesn't like sugar.'

This remark was received in silence. Her mother had decided not to go on at her about her imaginary animals, at least for the present. Her father was reading the paper and no one knew what he heard, or didn't hear, on these occasions. As for Terry, he accepted Jessie and her queer ways as being perfectly normal.

Three times Clover and Jessie had a glorious early morning ride. Jessie's confidence increased every time. She never thought of the possibility of being bucked off. The idea of a full gallop was taking its place, with Clover's hoofs thundering and the rush of cool air in her face.

On the fourth occasion when she got up early, to see the

sun shining and hear the birds singing, a disappointment awaited her. All the horses had gone, Clover too. The paddock was empty. She roamed up and down, unhappily, and even finding seven fine field mushrooms was not much comfort, though she enjoyed her share when her mother cooked them for breakfast.

'No horses at all,' she reported sadly.

'Oh, I forgot to tell you,' said her father. 'I saw Mr Spencer yesterday and the horses are being grazed nearer Bywell where their owner lives. It will be more convenient. They'll be taking part in a number of local point-to-points in a few weeks.'

Jessie looked for Clover every day, but never saw her. She talked to Terry about it. He was a very down-to-earth person but satisfying as a confidant. He always listened and he always said *something*, never a vague 'I don't know' or a rude 'So what?'

'Can you see her, Terry?'

Terry's intent gaze swept the entire field slowly. Jessie felt that he hadn't missed a square foot.

'No, I can't. And remember, I never did see her properly. Only something white that seemed to be alive.'

'Why do you think she had to go when the chestnuts went away?'

Terry pondered. 'I don't suppose she *had* to go. Maybe she wanted to go. You're the expert on horses, not me, but don't they hate being left alone?'

'Of course,' agreed Jessie. 'Some horses mind terribly. Even the chestnuts whinnied with joy if a horse passed along the lane, and galloped along their side of the hedge as near as possible to the other horse. When Clover's companions went, so did she. You've probably found the explanation.'

'Jessie,' said Terry, aiming his catapult at the elm tree under which the horses used to shelter, and hitting it, 'you know your white pony isn't real, don't you? Isn't alive like the chestnuts?'

'Of course I do, silly. She's a ghost.'

'Then she must be the ghost of a real pony who lived round here. We're newcomers and don't know much about the village. Why not ask someone? You needn't say why you want to know. In fact, much better not. People might think you're round the bend and avoid you.'

' 'Course I'll be careful and not let on. But who can I ask? I don't much like Mr Spencer. He says if I were a wench of his he'd find a job to fill my time. As if time needed filling. It's brimfull to start with. And he says: "Would you like to come and see my bull? He's a fine fellow." '

'And wouldn't you? I thought you were crazy about animals,' remarked Terry.

'But not animals with rings in their noses. They terrify me. I believe he knows I'm terrified.'

'There's no need to ask Mr Spencer. Who else is there? The lady at the village shop? The post woman? The man at the petrol pumps?'

'None of them sound right.'

'If you're so hard to please, think of someone yourself. Gosh! I hit that far post! I'm a wizard shot. I wish there were catapulting competitions. I bet I'd win.'

'Then you'd be Mr World and be on telly. What a hope!'

'It's more likely than you'd ever be Miss World, with all those freckles and your snub nose!'

That evening, in the middle of a game of canasta, Terry suddenly called out: 'The blacksmith!'

'Terry, you're wonderful,' cried Jessie, understanding perfectly what he meant. 'Just the very person. And he likes

THE PHANTOM ROUNDABOUT

children. There are always some standing round the forge, watching him shoe a horse. I'll go tomorrow. It's the last day of the holidays, anyhow.'

The next day found Jessie sauntering near the forge. There was no horse being attended to just then, which was convenient, as she didn't want an audience. Mr Bowls watched her out of the corner of his eye.

'Come closer, lass, if you have a mind. I'm making a firescreen for the folk at the hall. This is the design, on this bit of paper.'

'It's lovely, Mr Bowls. It's like the rays of the rising sun. Isn't it difficult after horseshoes?'

'It is and it isn't. Horseshoes have to be just so because they're made for a living creature. I want him to feel at home in his new shoes, just as your mother wants you to be comfortable in *your* new shoes. And you can complain if they pinch, better than he can.'

'Mr Bowls, have you lived here for a long time?'

'Fifty-nine years. I was born in the forge cottage. My father was a blacksmith and taught me the trade, and his father taught him.'

'And will you teach your son?'

'I had but one little laddie and he's in yon churchyard. But I had two bonny lasses and I've three grandsons.'

'Will one of your grandsons learn the trade?'

'We'll see. One wants to be a lorry driver and the other a pilot. And the third can't talk yet. He's a babbie.'

They stood in silence, Mr Bowls hammering on his anvil and Jessie watching him.

'Mr Bowls,' said Jessie, at last, 'was there ever a white pony in the village, perhaps one that grazed in our paddock?'

'That there was. A beautiful little creature. I knew her when I was first learning the trade. Come to think of it, the first shoe I ever made myself was for her. Proper proud, I was. Proud as Punch.'

'Tell me about her, please. Tell me all about her.'

'She belonged to the little girl who lived in your house, named Myrtle. No pony was ever better cared for. She was loved and exercised and groomed and fed titbits. They used to ride round the village and they always stopped at the forge for a chat. We all loved Myrtle and her pony. You remind me of her a little – long plaits, she had. But hers were golden. Then the family moved to France, something to do with the father's work, and the house was sold. And the pony, Snowy, was sold too. The new owners had a little girl who promised she'd take good care of Snowy. But that was a sad day's work — a sad day's work, if ever there was one.'

Mr Bowls was silent for so long that Jessie began to feel uneasy. Then she plucked up courage to ask:

'Please tell me the rest of the story. I'd really like to know. That is, if it's not too sad to tell.'

'Well, that new girl was a whited sepulchre. She rode Snowy too fast and too far, never sparing the whip. She didn't bother to have her shod, so her feet got proper sore. Sometimes she forgot to water her. Sometimes she never went near her for days on end, and of course Snowy pined. Any pony with a loving heart would have done the same. Myrtle had impressed on the new girl that the yew hedge at the bottom of the garden must be kept low, so the pony couldn't reach it. She, herself, used to trim it and put a layer of wire netting along the top as an extra precaution. But this other one soon forgot. The netting was taken away and used for something else, and the yew sprouted up. Snowy was half starved in winter (not even a bale of hay was thrown to her), and she cropped some of the yew and was poisoned and died. It's my belief she'd have died anyhow. Her heart was broken.

'The snow was on the ground the day she died. I don't mind admitting I shed a few tears myself when the vet told us. I was a bit of a softie. Still am.'

'How dreadful, Mr Bowls. Poor, poor Snowy. Did that horrid girl have another pony afterwards?'

'Yes. A hunter, and he threw her and so he was sold. And a blessing too.'

Jessie walked home full of thought, chiefly about the wickedness of the world.

A year later, and many riding lessons later, Jessie was

given a pony of her own. She had begged for a white one, but the only suitable one available was grey. She was called Mist. The blacksmith pronounced her a grand little pony when Jessie took her to visit him.

Sometimes, particularly in the early morning, Jessie saw Snowy and Mist playing together. Once they seemed to be nibbling each other's mane, lovingly. So they must have become friends.

Jessie wrote a poem about Snowy, but showed it only to Terry who declared it was as good as Wordsworth's Daffodils, which he had been learning at school.

THE GHOST PONY

Whiter than moonbeams,
Lighter than snows,
Free as blown thistledown,
The ghost pony goes.

No need for food or drink,
Bridle or rein,
Only a loving hand
Fondling her mane.

Tender your long-lashed eye,
Fragrant your breath,
You who have slipped from
The halter of death.

Lay them Straight

The Scott family thought as little of moving house as most people would think of changing bedrooms. The four children had been born in four different houses, though there was only a year or two between them in age. Ben was born in Scotland, Bill in Wales, Poppy in London and Primrose in Cornwall. Now they were moving again, to a house in the country, in North Yorkshire.

The children welcomed another move as, this time, they were to have a garden. The garden was a reality, but its size was not exactly known. This did not stop Ben and Bill laying out an imaginary cricket pitch; Poppy hoped for a pony in the paddock; and Primrose modestly expected a swing and a slide.

Mr Scott took little interest in the proceedings as he was going to America for a year, and Mrs Scott, as usual, was far too occupied with curtains that had already been lengthened, (or shortened) and now must be lengthened, (or shortened) yet again.

For a change, they arrived at the new house in brilliant sunshine. Before the furniture vans were completely empty, the children were prowling upstairs and downstairs, and in and out, getting in everybody's way, to find out 'what the other people had left behind'.

This was often a profitable exercise. At one new house they had found a hammock in the roof, rather ragged, but quite usable. At another, some toy soldiers were stuck behind a shelf. At a third, a chest expander had been overlooked, which, in spite of hours of practice, hadn't expanded the boys' chests in the slightest degree.

'Get out!' said their usually placid mother. 'Get out of my sight, all of you. I'll call you when—' she hesitated. 'I'll call you sometime,' she added.

'When it's teatime,' said Bill hopefully.

'Yes. That's right. Go and sweep up the straw that's blowing everywhere, or pull up a few of the thousand weeds in the garden.'

She gave these suggestions with no hope that they would be acted on. In fact, the children had noticed neither a straw nor a weed.

'What luck?' asked Poppy, as they lay on their backs on the lawn, among the daisies.

'Four walking-sticks in the downstairs cloakroom,' reported Bill.

'Some rusty croquet hoops in the shed,' said Primrose. 'No mallets, worse luck.'

'I know,' said Ben, leaping up. 'Let's put the croquet hoops in the lawn and use the walking-sticks for mallets.'

'Who's got a ball?'

'This will do,' said Bill, producing an old tennis ball from his pocket. 'Fetch the hoops, Primrose.'

The ground was so hard that the hoops had to be hammered in with a stone from the rockery. The game was played according to impromptu rules, made up as they went along. But like real croquet, it roused the baser passions. There were cries of: 'You cheated, you beast!' 'You moved the ball with your foot!' 'I won't play if I don't have another turn.' Players threw down their sticks and stalked off to sulk, though this seldom lasted more than a few minutes. The game was too good to miss.

When their mother called them, the removal men had gone, and on the kitchen table was a large teapot, half a fruit cake and some cheese. They showed their mother the four walking-sticks.

She looked at them carefully. 'They're nice,' she said, 'and the bands round each are real silver. They're named, too. Ben, you look. I really need my glasses and heaven knows where they are.'

Ben took them to the window. 'George,' he read. 'Godfrey, Giles and what looks like Gar-eth.'

'Gareth,' said his mother. 'From *Idylls of the King*. They sound rather Victorian names. I must ring up Mrs James and find out if she wants them sent on. They're old and may be of some value.'

She added 'Ring Mrs J.' to a long list of things to be done, pinned on the kitchen door.

'Did you ever ring Mrs James?' asked Poppy, some days later.

'Yes, I did, and she was most peculiar. Abrupt, almost rude. Not at all what she was like when she showed Daddy and me round the house.'

'But did she say she wanted the walking-sticks?'

'No. She said: "Keep them for God's sake. I never want to see them again", or something like that.'

'Now whatever did she mean?' said Poppy. 'They were hanging, good as gold, on four pegs in the cloakroom. Not harming a soul.'

'The only reason I can think of,' said Primrose, 'is that she was terribly house-proud and polished the silver bits twice a week. And she was just fed up.'

'She wasn't house-proud where dust was concerned,' said

Mrs Scott. 'I got black as a sweep just hanging the curtains. Anyhow, you can keep the sticks. So that's settled.'

That evening, with the help of the unwanted sticks, the children invented a game of golf with two-pound jam jars sunk in the ground for holes. It was even better than croquet and much more peaceful. Tempers stayed even.

'We'll keep the walking-sticks in the umbrella stand with the tennis rackets,' said Mrs Scott. 'It's stupid hanging them on pegs when we've hardly enough room for coats and macs.'

'Right-o,' said Poppy. 'But we found them there. It wasn't our idea in the first place.'

So the sticks found a home in the umbrella stand which was not a real stand, just a large, brown, Ali-Baba pot. When Primrose was little, the others threatened to drop her inside it, and indeed had done so, once or twice, when she was being a nuisance.

'I said keep those walking-sticks out of the way,' said Mrs Scott, a few days later, vacuuming briskly in the hall. 'They look so silly hanging in a row.'

'But I didn't—' began Ben.

'I certainly didn't—' put in Bill.

'I never touched them,' said Poppy.

'I never touch *anything*,' added Primrose indignantly.

'If you mean you never put anything away in its right place, that's a true word,' said her mother. 'Anyhow, I've put the walking-sticks back in the jar, and that's where they're going to stay. And I've hung up your anoraks and raincoats on the pegs in a row. They look so nice and tidy,' she added wistfully, knowing from past experience that this arrangement would probably be short lived.

A little later, the children were shocked to hear a note of real distress in their mother's voice. She was standing by the cloakroom door.

'Look! Look, all of you! All your clothes thrown on the floor and those blessed walking-sticks hanging on the pegs. Have you all gone crazy? It's the first time we've ever had a cloakroom with pegs and you turn it into a – into a shambles.'

The children's denials were more emphatic than before.

'We shouldn't dream of doing such a daft thing.'

'We're not as crazy as all that.'

'I hardly ever even go into the cloakroom.'

'Really mother, you can't honestly believe it's our fault?'

'I suppose the sticks jumped out of the jar and unhooked your clothes and hooked themselves on the pegs instead?'

'Perhaps they did,' said Poppy seriously.

The children started at their new schools in September, the fifth school for the boys, and the third for little Primrose, who was seven. At half-term, Mrs Scott suggested that they all went blackberrying. The children agreed as they at once saw their baskets full of fruit and Mrs Scott let her mind dwell pleasantly on shelves of blackberry jelly and supper tables adorned with large, juicy pies. She prudently took one of the walking-sticks with her to pull down any high branches. The children didn't want the trouble of carrying anything except their baskets, and these they kept throwing in the air and catching.

It was a good blackberry year and the five pickers did well, and came home satisfied, begging their mother, if she had time, to make a pie that very evening.

'I want bread-and-milk and blackberries and then I'll be like Flopsy, Mopsy and Cottontail,' said Primrose.

'That's easy enough,' said Mrs Scott, 'though I've never made any bread-and-milk before. It sounds easier than a pie.' Then she suddenly broke off. 'Oh dear, I haven't brought my stick home. I remember propping it up by the last gate, and

it must still be there. Will one of you boys run back and fetch it?'

Ben opened the cloakroom door and said in a queer, strained voice: 'There's no need to go back, is there?'

They all crowded to the door. The four sticks hung in their original places, one on each peg.

'But I *know* I took a stick, I *know* I did.'

'Of course you did, Mother, and we all know it, too. What we don't know, is how the stick got back,' said Ben.

'Who did it?' said Primrose. 'Who was it? A burglar? I don't think I like this house.'

Poppy put her arm round her and hugged her.

'We don't any of us understand, but there's an explanation,' said Mrs Scott firmly. 'There must be. There's an explanation for everything, if we could find it. I wish Daddy were here,' she added quietly.

'So do I,' said Primrose eagerly. She still believed her father knew everything about everything. 'Write to him tonight and ask him. Send it air mail.'

'She always does,' said Ben mechanically.

'There are things we'll never know and this is one of them,' said Bill.

'You mean ghosts?' Primrose's voice shook. 'I don't want to live in a house with a ghost. I won't ever go to sleep again because if I do I might dream of it. Let's go to a hotel.'

'Stop it, Bill. You're old enough to know better than to frighten your sisters.' Mrs Scott took Primrose on her lap and stroked her hair. 'Now we'll not talk of it again today. Just pick over the blackberries in that bowl and I'll get some frozen pastry out of the fridge. Perhaps we'll all feel better after a blackberry supper.'

That night, no one got to sleep quickly. They had all agreed, without words, to hang their clothes on the upper, less convenient, pegs. No one wished to disturb the walking-sticks again or arouse their displeasure. There they stayed for weeks, George and Godfrey and Giles and Gareth, with their silver bands unpolished.

But when the snow came, after Christmas, they took the sticks down to see if they would act as ski sticks.

'I've got Godfrey,' said Ben.

'I've got Giles,' said Bill.

'I've got poor old George,' said Poppy.

'And I must have Garter,' said Primrose. 'Oh, all right, Gareth. I've never heard of Gareth before.'

When the children came in from the snow, and took off their wellingtons, Ben collected the sticks.

'I'll hang them up,' he said, and did so.

Afterwards he whispered to Bill: 'I've done an experiment. I've changed the order. I've put Gareth first, then Godfrey, then Giles and George last. Let's see how they like that! And don't tell the girls or worry Mother.'

The next morning the boys went to see the result of their experiment. Ben examined them first.

'Just as I thought, Bill. They've gone back to their old order, George first and Gareth last. Don't let's tell Mother. She's worried enough as it is – worried sick. This would make her feel even worse. If only we could find out why this happens.'

'And how,' added Bill, 'and when.'

'We'll never find out by ourselves. The secret, if there is a secret, is nothing to do with us. It's in the past. Mother thought that Gareth was a Victorian name, copied from Tennyson's *Idylls of the King*. We must try to find someone pretty old who knew this house before Mrs James had it. Mother said she'd been here about twenty-five years.'

'Some people stay in one house for ages – for a lifetime,'

said Bill. 'It's only people like us who keep moving. But I hope we stay here for ages too, ghost and all. It isn't everyone who lives in a haunted house.'

'No, it isn't,' agreed Ben. 'And the ghost seems so harmless. He's just got this thing about order.'

'Some people are born tidy,' said Bill.

'I don't think any of our family were, thank goodness,' said Ben. 'Even mother's always losing her glasses and her shopping list.'

The boys did nothing at once for the simple reason that they could not think of anything to do. Time passed quickly with school occupying five days of the week, and Ben playing for the Under Twelves at rugger, and Bill a reserve. Mrs Scott occasionally dusted the walking-sticks, returning them scrupulously to their proper places.

In the Easter holidays, at their father's suggestion, their mother bought them a set of ordnance maps of the district and the boys spent most of the daylight hours exploring on their bicycles. But they often discussed the mystery as they rode along, or pushed their bicycles up one of the many hills.

'Let's ask at the post office,' said Bill. 'Post offices know everything.'

They had to wait their chance, as both preferred to be alone when they made their inquiries. One wet afternoon, they found the post office invitingly empty.

'Mrs Tongs,' said Ben boldly, 'can you tell us anything about the history of our house?'

She looked puzzled. 'I knew Mr and Mrs James who were there twenty years or more, till Mr James died last year.'

'Did either of them use a walking-stick?'

'Bless you, no. Hearty, they both were, working in the garden in all weathers and upright, too. They hardly ever used an umbrella, let alone a stick. Mr James was lifting his new potatoes when he dropped down dead. A sad loss to the village.'

'But who lived there before the James's?'

'I don't rightly remember as it was before my time, but I believe it was a military gentleman. A Colonel something – Hughes or Hawes. He was most peculiar, I've heard. Never spoke to anyone and sent his housekeeper to do all the shopping. Now *she's* the one you want to ask. She was with him till he died and I heard that he'd left her a nice little nest egg. Not that that wasn't right and proper. She deserved it, bearing with his tempers and tantrums. She lives in the next village – Tolby. Her name is Mrs Bell.'

The boys thanked her and set off for Tolby through the rain, which soon stopped, being only an April shower. They consulted the directory in the first telephone box they came to and found that T. E. Bell lived at Ford Cottage.

Ford Cottage was a neat, pretty little house, with a stream running by. At this point they had not made up their minds who should speak first, or what they should say, but luck was on their side. The front door opened, as they were propping up their bicycles, and a white-haired old lady came out, wearing gardening gloves, and carrying a rubber mat to kneel on. She saw the two boys looking over the gate, and smiled.

'What a lovely garden,' said Ben politely.

'And how beautifully kept,' added Bill.

'Do you like gardening yourselves?' she said hopefully.

'Well, we never do any,' admitted Ben.

'There are so many other things to do at your age,' went on Mrs Bell sympathetically. 'Do you live far away?'

'No, only a few miles,' said Ben. 'We moved into Holly Grange last summer.'

THE PHANTOM ROUNDABOUT

'Holly Grange,' Mrs Bell's expression changed to one of surprise. 'How very odd. That's where I lived for thirty years.'

'We knew that,' said Bill impulsively. 'That's really why we're here. We wanted to ask you some questions—' He paused, suddenly feeling like a policeman in a novel. He tried again: 'We wondered if you could give us some information—'

That sounded even worse.

'We wanted you to help us. You're the only person who can.'

'Come in and have a cup of tea,' said Mrs Bell warmly. 'I don't often have two young men to visit me. Though I know a good deal about boys. You see – I almost brought up four myself.'

'Your sons?' asked Ben.

'Oh no, dear. I was never married. But in my young days cooks and housekeepers often called themselves "Mrs", it gave us a certain standing, or so we thought. I daresay it was silly of us, but that's what we believed. No, I applied for the position of housekeeper as "Mrs Bell", and they engaged me. Colonel and Mrs Haigh, I mean.'

'I suppose Mrs Haigh went out to work as she needed a housekeeper,' suggested Bill.

'Oh no, nothing like that. The Colonel was much older than his wife. He'd seen service in India and other eastern countries, and he married her when he retired. He was more than old enough to be her father. She was hardly out of the schoolroom, pretty as a picture and gentle as a dove. She had four sons in four years and then her health broke down. She was never robust at the best of times. I was engaged to run the house and take care of the children, and I did as well as I could. Two years later, when Master Gareth was just learning to walk, she died. And then, naturally, I took her place. The Colonel never married again. She was the light of his life.'

'Were they nice little boys?' inquired Ben.

'Yes, they were, and utterly devoted to each other. The Colonel was a hard, strict father and believed firmly in discipline, but they escaped when they could and did the things ordinary boys like doing – climbing trees and fishing and making dens.'

'Was the Colonel cruel?'

'No, not cruel, though I often thought him so. He wouldn't let them wear gloves, and they had to have cold baths even in the middle of winter, and he thought sweets and cakes were bad for them. He was determined they should grow up tough and hardy.'

'And did they?'

'They did and they didn't. Their poor hands were covered with chilblains, but they never complained – or not to their father. I used to creep into their rooms at night and rub salve on their red, swollen fingers. They went to boarding school when they were seven, and I used to send them tuck, chocolate and home-made cakes, though of course it had to be a secret. They called me Ellie, as Gareth called me that before he could speak properly, and soon they were all calling me Ellie.'

'Didn't they have any fun with their father?'

'Only in the open air, sometimes. They were too frightened of him to have fun indoors. He took them kite-flying and walking and cycling. He was very fit for a man of his age. They had to do everything in the right order – the Colonel rode along first, then George, then Godfrey, then Giles, then Gareth last. Gareth was always small and delicate and Mrs Haigh had chosen his name from some book of poetry that she often read; by Lord Tennyson, I think she said. I believe the Colonel knew she wasn't long for this world and he tried to please her by letting her choose the baby's name. Highfalutin', *he* called it.'

'Didn't they rebel when their father was so beastly?' asked Ben, his eyes flashing.

'Oh no. How could they? They were only children and had no relations to go to. Neither the Colonel nor Mrs Haigh had brothers or sisters. They made plans to run away from home, but the older ones wouldn't go without the little ones. They just had me and I dared not go against his orders too much or he might have dismissed me. Then what would have happened to them?'

'I see. They were helpless.'

'Of course, they had fun among themselves as children will. The Colonel intended them all to be soldiers when they grew up, but their minds were set on quite different careers. The two eldest were musical, like their dear mother, and Giles wanted to be an architect, and Gareth wanted to be an artist. I've still got drawers full of pictures he painted.'

'Mrs Bell,' said Ben, laying down his slice of chocolate cake. 'Mrs Bell, what about the four walking-sticks?'

Mrs Bell, hitherto so talkative, became suddenly silent. She busied herself with poking the fire.

'So that's why you're here,' she said at last. 'Now I understand. The Colonel gave each boy a walking-stick, engraved with his name, on his eighteenth birthday. They came from some special shop in York. Gareth's eighteenth birthday came in the winter, in January, and the whole family went for a holiday somewhere in Switzerland. The Colonel was almost past mountain walking – he was over seventy – and he felt the cold dreadfully after his long years in the east – but still, he went.'

She paused.

'Don't tell us if you'd rather not,' said Ben.

'But I want to tell someone. I must tell someone. It's in my mind day and night since the accident happened. It was an unusually sunny day and the boys, well, the four young men, set out on an expedition to a glacier. I think it was a glacier. They wore their straw hats because the Colonel was frightened that they might get sun-stroke, about the only thing he was frightened of. Nowadays they'd have been dressed differently and equipped with ice-axes and goggles and climbing boots and the like, but things were different then. Even ladies went up mountains in long dresses and motor veils. No one knows exactly what happened, but from the position of the bodies, Gareth had slipped down a steep slope, and the other three had tried to save him. They made a human chain over the ice, linked by their out-stretched sticks. They might even have reached him, but an avalanche fell and they were buried. The coroner said they might have lived some time under the snow, but no one knew it had happened.

'It was days before they were found and then a rescue dog scratched away the snow and uncovered one of the sticks. They were buried in the little cemetery near the hotel, full of the graves of the climbers.'

'What happened to the old Colonel?' asked Bill.

'He was heart-broken, for the second time in his life. They say hearts can't break, but his did. He was a broken man. He lapsed into almost complete silence. I did all the shopping and communicating with the outside world. He brought the four walking-sticks back with him and kept the silver bands polished with his own hands. They hung where you probably found them, in a row on the lower pegs in the cloakroom. I soon discovered that they wanted – or someone wanted them – to stay that way.'

'Thank you very much, Mrs Bell. What a sad story.'

'What a good thing the boys had you to look after them.'

'Thank you for telling us. And for the tea.'

Ben and Bill got up to go.

'There's just one thing I left out,' went on Mrs Bell. 'The boys had all planned to leave home when they returned from Switzerland, to run away, in fact. They had taken two rooms in London and were going to get any job they could – clerking or even labouring, to start with. I was the only person who knew about it.'

'Didn't you want to go too? They were almost like your own children.'

'Yes, they were, but they were hers, and they had inherited

her loving heart. 'Stay with the old man, Ellie,' they said. 'He's getting very frail. We'll always keep in touch, whatever happens, and we'll write to Father when we've got jobs and have settled down.'

'And they do keep in touch in a way, don't they, through the walking-sticks?' said Ben. 'Wouldn't you like to have them back? Mother would gladly hand them over. She hates them.'

'You're kind boys,' said Mrs Bell, smiling. 'You can bring them round, one day. They'd be company.'

But when Ben and Bill got home, their mother told them the sticks were no longer there.

'A man came round this afternoon trying to buy antiques and I offered him the walking-sticks. He was interested in the silver bands and offered to pay me for them. But, of course, I didn't take any money. They're better out of the house. The girls were half-afraid to use the cloakroom.'

Through the Door

Maria was a fortunate little girl, and she knew this herself. Though she was an only child, and therefore a prey to the loneliness an only child experiences, she lived next door to such a large, warm, friendly family that she felt as though she had five brothers and sisters, instead of none.

Her closest friend was Clare, a girl of her own age, but Clare's four older brothers were important too. Mrs Cope, Clare's mother, often included Maria in family outings. She went with them to watch Jimmy in a swimming gala, and she joined in Paul's birthday treat which was a visit to an ice rink. Both Clare and she sometimes accompanied Charles on his bird-watching expeditions.

Charles took no notice of them, provided they lay perfectly still in the ditch, or reed bed, or wherever he had decreed they should freeze into immobility and silence. But they caught Charles' enthusiasm and felt it was all worth while to catch a glimpse of a green woodpecker or hear a grasshopper warbler.

Lance, the eldest, was already a man in Maria's eyes. He went to college, but was as kind-hearted as the rest of the family and he allowed Clare and Maria to sleep on the lawn in his new tent – after he had tried it out himself.

Then, out of the blue, came the terrible news that the Copes were leaving. Their house was up for sale and all was confusion and desolation. When the last furniture van drove off, Maria burst into the tears which she had been restraining for weeks. She felt that she would never be happy again. Every day she and Clare had run in and out of each other's house freely. Now all this had come to a dead stop. For ever.

But even weeping must stop at last, and Maria found she could go to bed without the tears starting again. She tried having other friends to tea, but there seemed nothing to do to pass the time. Then her parents gave her a small black kitten and Midge, as he was called, did more than anyone else to make her cheerful. He was a particularly cheerful kitten.

It was many months, not a few weeks as she had hoped, before the first, longed-for, visit to Clare could be arranged, as there had been so much to do to the new house. At last she found herself in a train leaving Liverpool Street for Ipswich, where some of the Cope family would meet her, and drive her the rest of the way. As she settled herself in the corner of the carriage she was very conscious that it was her first long train journey alone, and though she felt excited rather than apprehensive, she was not relaxed as she would have been on a familiar bus ride.

She looked out of the window and tried to remember all she had heard about the new house from conversation or letters. Clare was a writer of long, detailed, many-paged letters that became creased and crumpled with many re-readings.

It had once been a small Elizabethan manor which had been much restored and modernized over the years. 'It's just a shell,' Lance said, 'with massive chimneys and a few original windows.'

'It's nothing if not old,' said Mrs Cope, 'with uneven floors and draughts, but it seemed to suit us. We liked the views and the garden and it just holds us all when everyone's home.'

'You're to share my bedroom,' Clare had written, 'and it's

the best room in the house, with a secret staircase. I won't tell you any more as you'll soon see for yourself. But we can talk as long as we like in bed. No one knows what we are up to. It's a private room, and that's something I've never had before. My last bedroom had a fanlight and someone always noticed if I ever tried to read late.'

The moment she got out of the train at Ipswich, all sense of loss and absence melted away. The Copes were just exactly the same, but even nicer, such of them as had come to meet her. Mrs Cope greeted her as if she were a long-lost daughter, and Clare hugged and kissed her too. It was a real homecoming.

Charles carried her suitcase upstairs and told her, seriously, that she might hear a bittern booming if she were lucky. Clare hurried ahead and opened a door.

'We can manage now, Charles. I want to show Maria the rest of the house myself. Look, Maria, these wooden stairs are just for me. They only lead to my bedroom, well, to our bedroom now you're here. They're rather steep and slippery, or so I thought when I first went up them. But they seem ordinary enough now. Take care.'

Maria did find the narrow stairs steep and awkward and she felt inwardly glad that she was not going to sleep by herself, wherever they led. It was all too private, too strange, to her mind.

'All this is my very own,' said Clare triumphantly, as she flung open another narrow door at the top of the stairs. They went into a long, narrow, attic room, with low beams across the sloping ceiling. It was the oddest room that Maria had ever seen. Once it must have been dark and gloomy, a place of shadows and secrets. Now it had two large windows at floor level, and two beds with brightly coloured counterpanes, and several pieces of furniture that Maria remembered from the old house. A white painted chest of drawers. Several white chairs. A red toy box and a new desk and chair. All this Maria saw in the first few seconds. Other details she noticed afterwards.

'You've got a new desk. How lovely!'

'Yes. Mummy wanted me to be really comfy and quiet up here. I can do my prep if I want. Or write to you. She said the boys and their possessions spread all over the old house and it was time I had a room of my own, if I wanted to be out of everybody's way.'

'And do you ever want to be up here alone?'

'Sometimes I do and then it's bliss. Jimmy plays the same record for hours and hours and nearly drives us all mad and they all have their friends in more. That's because we live in the country. But I often do things downstairs with everyone else. It's nice being able to choose.

'This is the oldest bit of the house,' she went on. 'Or so Lance says. He knows more about the place than anyone else. He says this is part of the original house. Come here. I'll show you.'

Clare opened a door at one end of the room and Maria peered inside. It was a long, low, oddly shaped cupboard and would have been pitch dark without a small, sloping skylight. It was now fitted out with hooks and a rail for coat-hangers. Clare's clothes hung there looking rather lost.

'There's lots of room for you and spare coat-hangers. Use what you want when you unpack.'

Maria unpacked and put her clothes in the secret cupboard. Then the girls went down to tea. The stairs seemed steeper than ever now Maria was going down them. She clung to the handrail every step of the way.

After tea, Maria said she must write a birthday card for her mother, which she had brought with her.

'Write it at my desk,' said Clare. 'You'll find stamps and everything you want.'

'All right. I will.'

Maria liked the idea of using the new desk. She found her way up to the landing and opened the door that led to the stairs. As she went into the room, she was surprised to find she was not alone. She heard no definite sound, but she knew someone had followed her into the attic. She turned round quickly. Close behind her, only a foot or so away, was another girl. This other girl showed no surprise. She seemed so calm and composed that it might have been her room, and Maria the intruder. She was tall and pale, wearing a striped dress, and carrying a pewter plate and mug.

'Who are you?' asked Maria.

'I'm Tabitha.' She offered no apology or explanation for her presence. Maria felt even more like a trespasser.

'What – what are you doing?' She looked at the plate and the mug. Tabitha looked slightly surprised at this obvious question and raised her eyebrows, but she replied gently:

'Taking Father Simon his supper.'

Then, to Maria's horror and amazement, Tabitha and her plate walked right through the solid wooden door of the hanging cupboard, and disappeared. Maria fancied she heard the faint murmur of two voices, Tabitha's clear, childish one and a man's deeper tone. She did not wait to hear more, but fled to the comfort of the ground floor. She skimmed down the steep stairs as if in a dream, not feeling the wooden treads. Something in her face brought Clare quickly to her side.

'Are you all right? What is it?'

'Can we talk somewhere?' whispered Maria. 'Now.'

'I'll just show Maria the garden,' said Clare loudly, and taking her friend's arm she hurried her out of doors. Maria

only waited for the door to close behind them to say urgently:

'Clare, I saw something. I saw a ghost in your room. I know I did. I'm certain.'

'Was it a fair haired girl?'

Maria's face fell, but she reacted instantly.

'Oh Clare, so you knew all the time. Why ever didn't you tell me if you knew about her? How could you just leave me alone to discover her for myself? We used to share everything.'

Clare squeezed her arm and said warmly:

'It wasn't really a bit like that. Of course I was going to tell you about the ghost – I was longing to – but we've hardly had a minute together since you arrived, without other people milling around. It was rather sad, or so I think now. I once passed a girl with fair hair on the secret staircase. We neither of us said a word. I was far too frightened to speak first. I looked back and saw her reach the door into the attic and just pass through it like air, and disappear.'

'Did you tell anyone?'

'I told Mummy and she told Daddy. They were both very serious and disbelieving. They explained so patiently that I couldn't have seen anything, because there wasn't anything there. When they heard I'd looked back and seen the girl on the stairs they said that proved the whole thing was impossible as it would have been too dark. They went on and on showing me how impossible it was. Then they suggested I swopped rooms with one of the boys if I thought I might feel creepy up there alone.'

'What did you say?' asked Maria.

'Of course I refused. I knew that Jimmy would change with me like a flash, but I wasn't going to give up my lovely bedroom for anything. I said perhaps I'd imagined it and just laid low. I rather think they may have forgotten about it by now.'

'But you haven't forgotten?'

'No, and I never will.'

The girls had a cheerful evening playing a new card game with Jimmy and Paul which involved a great deal of shouting and laughing and slapping down of cards. They went to bed quickly and neither mentioned ghosts. Clare only said as she got into bed:

'The bedside lamp is between us. You just press this to put it on. And the main switch is in the corner.'

'Thanks,' said Maria, snuggling down.

For three days nothing happened that wasn't pleasant and ordinary and like old times. They bird-watched with Charles. Cycled miles down the quiet lanes with Maria on one of the boys' old bicycles. Went shopping. Had a winter picnic. Then, on the third night, Maria woke up and breathed deeply. She smelt a queer unusual smell. In a second she was wide awake.

'Clare, wake up, do! I think the house is on fire.'

She stretched out an arm and shook Clare, screaming in her ear. Clare woke.

'What's wrong? Are you ill?'

'No. Just smell. Smell hard. Is it smoke?'

'Let's put the light on.'

The both groped for the button on the lamp, but though it was only a few inches away neither could find it. Maria jumped out of bed and felt for the main switch, but her fingers scrabbled on plain wall. That had vanished too. Choking with terror she found her way to Clare's bed and clung to her. Then came the tinkle of a little bell.

The air cleared and they found the switch for the light. Everything was quiet and normal except for a very faint odour, so faint that it seemed to come and go as they breathed.

'Nothing's on fire,' said Clare comfortingly. She opened the door at the top of the stairs. 'No smell coming up. You poor, poor thing. Did you dream we were being burned alive?'

'There was something peculiar,' insisted Maria. 'It woke me. It nearly choked me. Then, when the little bell rang, it seemed to go. It reminds me of something.'

They soon fell asleep and in the morning, when Mrs Cope asked if they had had a good night, they looked at each other before answering. Then Clare said:

'It would have been good if Maria hadn't dreamed the house was on fire, and shouted in my ear. We soon got off again.'

The next night it was Clare who woke, but not in terror. She touched Maria gently and whispered:

'Open your eyes and keep quiet.'

Maria opened sleepy eyes and saw, at once, that the room was no longer dark. At the far end of the attic, furthest from their beds, was a faint glow. It was the soft, flickering light of several candles. A company of strangely dressed people were gathered in silence before a table spread with a white cloth, with a silver cross above it. Both girls knew it to be an altar. A dark robed priest murmured some words in an unfamiliar tongue. There was the tinkle of a bell. The priest raised his arms. The same queer smell pervaded the room.

'Incense,' breathed Clare.

Maria nodded.

Then came a great thundering outside and a pounding on a wooden door. There was shouting and they heard the words: 'We are betrayed. The Queen's men are at hand.'

At once all was dark. The candles had been blown out instantly. They heard the confused sounds of feet, of furniture being moved, of muffled orders. It was like a rapid scene shifting, well rehearsed. Both girls felt for the switch of the lamp and one of them found it. Light sprang up and they saw, at a glance, that the scene at the far end of the attic had changed. People – candles – altar – silver cross – all had vanished. The dolls' house and the toy chest were back in their places, with the rugs and pictures.

The knocking had stopped and the voices were quiet, but the room still seemed to echo with the thud, thud, on the heavy door.

Though the girls had not been involved in the strange scene, except as spectators, they were both thoroughly disturbed. Their hearts beat quickly and when Clare whispered: 'Let's get out of here,' her voice sounded husky and unnatural, as if her throat were dry. They slid rather than ran down the steep stairs, clinging tightly to the banister, and when they were both safely on the landing, they burst through the nearest door. To Maria it was literally any door as she had not sorted out the various rooms on that floor, and to Clare it meant only that it was the nearest.

It turned out to be Lance's room. He woke at the click of the old-fashioned latch, and switched on his bedside lamp, apparently wide awake in an instant.

'What on earth are you two doing in the middle of the night?' he inquired calmly. 'Have you seen a ghost?'

'Oh Lance,' said Clare thankfully, 'that's just what we have seen. Several ghosts.'

'Both of you?' asked Lance.

'Yes. Both of us together.'

'If two people have seen a ghost it deserves investigation,' went on Lance. 'Serious investigation. And if the ghosts were plural it's even more serious. But we may as well investigate in comfort.'

He turned on the electric fire, and indicated that they were both to sit down on the sofa, and he took his eiderdown off his bed and tucked it cosily over their knees. The warmth and comfort, and Lance's normal, matter-of-fact tone, worked wonders. Someone was taking them seriously, neither panicking nor doubting. Just listening and believing.

'Now tell me everything, every single thing.' Lance ran his fingers through his mop of hair, and sat down opposite, his elbows on his knees, and chin on his clasped hands.

'We smelt a funny smell,' said Maria, 'both of us.'

'It was incense,' corrected Clare, 'though I did not recognise it at first, but it was incense, I'm sure. We woke up, or rather I woke up, and nudged Maria. She woke at once, and we found the room wasn't dark and at the far end a service was going on.'

'It was a mass,' said Maria. 'They had a priest in white robes and a table made into an altar and a silver cross hanging above.'

'And they rang a little bell,' put in Clare, 'and chanted.'

'It was so secret and solemn,' went on Maria. 'It was beautiful and peaceful till the hammering on the door began, several people hammering with their fists and shouting.'

'It didn't seem to be on our ordinary door, either, not on the one we always use near our beds. It sounded as if it were at the far end of the room,' said Clare. 'What did you think, Maria?'

'Yes, it wasn't close enough to be on our door. You're right. The voices shouting the warning were far away too. A loud voice said: "We are betrayed. The Queen's men are here".'

'Not *here*,' corrected Clare. '*At hand*. The Queen's men are at hand. And then there was more knocking.'

'Yes, you're right, Clare. I remember now.'

Lance listened to every word and when there was a pause, he spoke:

'Queen Elizabeth the First was a Protestant and passed a law forbidding the saying of Mass. But many Catholic families made elaborate arrangements to worship in secret. There were Catholic carpenters about who, under cover of doing some alterations to the house, devised secret hiding places where a priest could be concealed. They were called priest holes. Then, usually at night, the priest ventured out to say the forbidden Mass and often neighbours and friends stole through the dark countryside to join them. Attics were sometimes changed into temporary chapels.'

'Where did they make the priest holes?' asked Clare.

'Oh, in secret cupboards and behind panelling and often in the chimney.'

'Wasn't it too hot for the poor priest?' inquired Maria.

'I don't think he *lived* in the chimney. It was a good hiding place if the Queen's men were on the prowl, searching out priests and disobedient Catholics. A man called Thomas Phillips, cunning as a fox, led the searches. He could decipher codes and his spies were everywhere, measuring buildings and tapping walls to find secret rooms.'

'What happened when the priests and the Catholics were caught?'

'The priests were often put to death and the Catholics heavily fined. They might be put to death as well.'

'Was my bedroom cupboard a priest hole?' asked Clare, her eyes never leaving Lance's face.

'It might easily have been. They were often built in gables. It might even have had an inner room to deceive the searchers. They wouldn't suspect another secret place if they'd found the first one.'

'Shall we investigate inside my cupboard and see what we can find? Let's start now.' Clare jumped up eagerly.

'Are you both agreed over what you've told me? Did either of you see or hear anything the other didn't?'

They shook their heads.

'Oh no, Lance. We were together so of course we saw the same things. And heard the same things. We were as wide awake as – well, as we are now.'

'Then what happened?' said Lance encouragingly.

'Then they swept everything away like lightning,' said Clare, 'or I suppose that's what they did. They blew out the candles first of all, so we couldn't watch what they were doing. They were so quick that they must have had lots of practice. They must have rehearsed it.'

'I do hope they weren't caught,' said Maria. 'They weren't doing any harm. There were some children at the service and Father Simon was like a real father, caring for his family.'

'Who was Father Simon?' asked Lance, quick as a flash. 'You haven't told me about him.'

Clare first, then Maria afterwards, related their earlier meetings with Tabitha, carrying Father Simon's supper.

'You hadn't mentioned Tabitha to Maria before she saw her herself?' asked Lance, addressing Clare.

'No, I told you I hadn't,' said Clare impatiently. 'I was longing to tell her but we hadn't been alone together for a minute. And she was much braver than me. She spoke to Tabitha and found out her name and actually asked her what she was doing.'

'I was a bit puzzled, but she seemed so real and ordinary,' explained Maria, 'except for her old fashioned clothes. I wasn't frightened. It was when she and her supper tray walked right through the cupboard door that I was scared. Then I knew she was someone different. A ghost, in fact.'

'You're lucky girls to see a ghost – lots of ghosts. I wish I'd had the chance,' said Lance. 'Now would you like to finish the night in my bed and I'll go up to the attic, or are you all right?'

The girls looked at each other, but neither wanted to be the first to admit she felt uneasy. Anyhow, there were two of them.

'I'll go back to my own bed, Lance, thank you,' said Clare.

'And so will I,' added Maria.

'O.K.,' said Lance cheerfully. 'You can leave your bedside lamp on for company, if you like, and I'll leave my door open. But I don't think you'll see or hear anything else tonight. If you do, just call and I'll be up the stairs in a jiffy.'

Though the girls were sure they would lie awake all night, it was only a few minutes before sleep overcame them. They heard nothing more till morning, not even Lance's bare feet as he padded upstairs to make sure they had dropped off. He, himself, puzzled and pondered between fitful dozes.

Though Lance and the girls had made no arrangements to keep the night's events to themselves, they did not mention them to the rest of the family. Lance had been more impressed than he had shown by Clare's determination to keep Tabitha's second appearance from her parents, once she had experienced their sympathetic disbelief, and had realized that the possession of her bedroom was at stake, the bedroom she prized so highly. He was also impressed by Maria's attitude. She's got her head screwed on the right way, he thought to himself. Only children aren't all soft and silly. She's a cool customer, for a start.

During the day, while the younger boys were out on their bicycles and Charles had disappeared with his binoculars, Lance invited the girls to come to his room, which was warm and comfortable, though small. The table was covered with books and papers as he often studied up there.

'I'll tell you a few facts I've collected about the time when this house was built. You'll see why, if you listen.'

They fixed their eyes on him, unwaveringly, and did not fidget or interrupt. An idea crossed his mind that he wouldn't mind teaching children, one day, if they listened like these two, absorbing every syllable.

'Yes, we might take some measurements later on. I don't think Dad would stand for any more walls being pulled down. The alterations have cost too much already. But he couldn't object to peaceful measuring and checking.'

By some mysterious process, never perfectly understood, the other boys were soon caught up in the possibility of there being a priest hole actually in the house, just waiting to be discovered. The children swarmed all over the building with rulers and tape measures, measuring every nook and cranny, and tapping the woodwork like demented woodpeckers, listening for a hollow sound. As they soon found out, many wooden surfaces gave back a hollow note if tapped often enough, with sufficient force. But Lance's respect for the fabric of the house kept them from using tools which could do damage.

'Stick to accurate measuring,' he advised. 'Be scientific. Write it all down. When we get a water-tight case for the existence of a priest hole, then that's the time for the next step. Let's be sure of our facts first.'

A black notebook was produced with PRIEST HOLES written on the cover, and all measurements, scientific or otherwise, were inscribed inside in Lance's spidery writing.

'Whatever the children are doing is keeping them quiet and out of the way,' said Mr Cope with satisfaction.

'It's all Lance,' said his wife. 'I never thought he took much notice of the younger ones, but I was wrong. Clare and Maria never willingly leave him alone. I heard he'd had to lock his door the other day to get some of his own work done.'

'He started the notion of a priest hole and now it's everyone's idea. They are all dead keen on finding one. They talk learnedly about secret masses and codes and hiding places,' went on Mr Cope. 'Just look at that!' He opened the window and stuck his head out.

'Don't lean out so far, Jimmy,' he shouted, as he looked upward.

'I'm all right, Daddy. Charles has got hold of my feet. I really believe I may be on to something.'

A steel measure waved wildly from a landing window.

'I've dropped it again. You go and fetch it, Charles. I can see it shining in that laurel bush.'

'Fetch it yourself. You let go of it.'

'But I fetched your biro last time you dropped it.'

'Fair's fair.'

Mr Cope withdrew his head and slammed the sitting room window shut.

If they could have listened to a conversation taking place in another part of the house, Mr and Mrs Cope would have been surprised.

'If only we knew that they weren't caught, that night, and that Father Simon wasn't killed,' said Maria. 'But we never shall. I asked Lance if there would be anyone on guard and he said yes, of course. There would always be a look-out. They might have given the warning in time. The sound of distant hoofs – a dog barking – an unexpected light – a little would have been enough to put them on the alert. After all, their lives were at stake.'

There was a pause. Then Clare spoke.

'We shan't see anything again, I know we shan't. It's happened. It won't happen again, ever. I keep wondering why you and I were given that ghostly glimpse of the past. We were so ignorant. So unsuitable.'

'Now I don't agree with you,' contradicted Maria. 'In one way we were very well chosen, apart from being actually on the spot. I think ghosts are often lonely. Tabitha must have felt very drawn to you, as a girl like herself, to allow herself to be seen at all. I was too surprised, as it happened, to be really scared so I was able to speak to her. And she replied quietly and naturally. It may have been many years since a living person spoke to her, poor girl. I've heard that ghosts only show themselves to people who believe in them.'

'I'm thankful I was frightened silently,' said Clare, who

couldn't forgive herself for being frightened at all. 'You always hear of people screaming and screeching when they see a ghost. Tabitha may not have known that I was petrified,' she went on more cheerfully. 'I didn't utter a word. I do so hope she didn't know, or guess.'

The two girls acquired a good knowledge of priests and priest holes. They read books lent by Lance, and Maria read many more when she got home, helped by a friendly librarian. But she kept discussion of their strange experiences for times, in the holidays, when she and Clare were together and never mentioned it to other friends or even to her parents. Over the years, Tabitha became an intimate and friendly figure in their memories, like someone met on a journey, and never forgotten.